Firing on the run...

The whole of the warehouse had erupted with noise as the automatic weapons sent streams of bullets winging in crisscross patterns. Manning and Encizo covered each other as they took turns reloading. The Phoenix warriors caught sight of Katz, alone inside the office enclosure. But a couple of Libyan terrorists were already moving in that direction, their weapons rising as they neared the open doorway.

Manning didn't hesitate. He broke away from Encizo, going on a prowl and tracking in on the closest Libyan. Just then, the Arab turned without warning and the muzzle of his AK-47 homed in on Manning.

The burly Canadian took a full-length dive to the floor, and he heard the crackle of the AK-47 above him. Rolling to a jarring stop, Manning set his sights and fired. The blast ripped the terrorist's throat out in an ugly red flash.

But even as the man slumped to his knees, his partner swiveled in Manning's direction, snarling defiance. He yanked the barrel of his AK-47 around, his finger tightening on the trigger...

Mack Bolan's
PHOENIX FORCE.

PHOENIX FORCE.

GAR WILSON

EXTREME PREJUDICE

A GOLD EAGLE BOOK FROM
WORLDWIDE.

TORONTO • NEW YORK • LONDON • PARIS
AMSTERDAM • STOCKHOLM • HAMBURG
ATHENS • MILAN • TOKYO • SYDNEY

First edition November 1990

ISBN 0-373-61350-4

Special thanks and acknowledgment to
Michael Linaker for his contribution to this work.

PROLOGUE

The icy chill of the Russian winter struck Leoni Testarov as he stepped from the warmth of the black Mercedes-Benz limousine. He slammed the door and paused for a moment to take in the stark scenery. Tall, gaunt trees thrust up into the bleak gray sky from which heavy flakes of snow drifted to earth. To his right, through the trees, Testarov could see the frozen surface of a lake.

The KGB major shivered despite his heavy overcoat. Impatiently he turned toward the imposing dacha outside which the car had dropped him. Testarov had seen many of the traditional Russian country houses, but the one before him put them all to shame. It was large and handsome, rich with carved wood and overhanging roof gables. From a chimney, smoke drifted thickly into the pale sky.

Not for the first time, the KGB operative asked himself why he had been summoned to the place. The request, which had merely served to thinly veil a direct order—had come via an extremely discreet route. Testarov had realised that it was no ordinary summons. He was being called to a high-level meeting that was apparently off-the-record.

Which explained the long drive from Moscow to such an isolated spot.

Testarov's curiosity was well aroused, and he was eager to find out exactly what was going on. He strode up to the dacha and knocked on the heavy door. It was opened almost immediately. A stern-faced man of indeterminate age gestured for Testarov to enter. As he stepped into the entrance hall, the door closed with a solid thud, shutting out the cold.

"Your coat, Major," the manservant said politely.

Testarov removed the heavy garment, and along with his gloves and fur hat, handed it over. The servant took the coat to a shallow alcove where hooks already held a number of coats. When he returned, he indicated with a courteous gesture that Testarov was to follow him. They crossed the entrance hall and walked along a wood-paneled passage to a pair of doors. The manservant opened the doors and stood to one side for the KGB man.

"Major Leoni Testarov."

Testarov stepped into the room, and behind him the doors closed silently. He remained standing just inside the doors, his eyes flicking around the room. It was long, with a low ceiling. Book-lined shelves covered much of the wall space. Where there were no books, oil paintings hung in gilt frames. Wall lights threw soft illumination across the carpeted floor. At the far end of the room stood a heavy desk, with a large curtained window behind it. The top of the desk was covered in tooled leather. On Testarov's left was a huge open fireplace, constructed from natural stone, with a polished wood mantle over it. Displayed above the fireplace was a collection of weapons—swords, sabres, handguns. They all looked old and valuable. A roaring log fire blazed in the wide hearth, throwing its welcome heat out across the room. Comfortable leather armchairs were arranged before the fireplace, and numerous bottles of wine and other drinks crowded a low table.

Three men were seated before the fire. Testarov knew two of them, but the third was a total stranger.

And he knew the one who rose to greet him very well.

"Come on in, Leoni, and sit down. What would you like to drink?"

"Hot coffee if you have it," Testarov said.

The host nodded. "A fresh pot is there on the hearth. Help yourself. Leoni, I believe you know Erik Kochak?"

"Yes, we have met before," Testarov said, acknowledging Kochak's presence by a nod and taking note of the fact that his host was in no hurry to introduce the unknown man.

Testarov poured himself a large cup and spooned in coarse brown sugar. He drank, grateful for the coffee's warmth.

"How was the drive from Moscow?" the host asked.

His name was Nikolai Gagarin, and he was a colonel in the KGB. Gagarin was a powerful man. His life was dedicated to the KGB. Its survival and its expansion. Both were on shaky ground at the moment. The Soviet hierarchy, in its bid to show a new face to the world, was doing some in-house pruning. One of its ploys was the reduction of KGB influence on the world scene. In its own defence the KGB had argued that its presence was still a requirement. The world remained a dangerous place, and there were still many enemies at large. An easing of global tension between the superpowers was not going to wipe away every bad thought directed toward the Soviet Union. Only a complete fool would believe that peace on earth was the watchword for the 1990s.

Testarov took another sip of Gagarin's rich coffee. "It was extremely long and boring," he said.

"Then you will have had ample time in which to reflect on your failure during that disastrous coup attempt in the Philippines."

Testarov glanced at the speaker.

Kochak was a KGB major with a personality problem, the problem being, in Testarov's opinion, that he had *no* personality. The man was a total nonentity when it came to the social graces. On the other hand, he possessed one of the finest strategic brains in the KGB. He was an excellent field operative, too. He had eliminated many people in the KGB cause. Kochak, despite his lack of charisma, was a good KGB man.

"I had plenty of time for that during my stay in hospital," Testarov snapped back.

"Major Testarov's courage is not under scrutiny here," Gagarin spoke up smoothly. "His case has already been examined and a decision reached. We all know what the committee decided. Their conclusion was accepted, and their rule is now in force. I will not hear further criticism of Major Testarov's involvement with the Philippine operation."

"May I say something?" Testarov interrupted.

"Of course, Leoni."

"The Philippine episode should serve as an example to us all," the KGB man said. "It proved to me personally, in retrospect, that such a complicated exercise should never have been contemplated. There were too many details to fit together. Too many agencies, all trying to reach a common goal. Let me say, however, that I am not trying to excuse the fact that I failed to carry out my part. But I was fortunate. At least I came out of it alive."

"Leoni is being modest, of course," Gagarin said. "Despite being severely wounded, he made it to the rendezvous point and was picked up by the submarine that was waiting. He underwent extensive surgery on board the submarine and had three more operations after he returned to Moscow. Even today he is still in pain. His refusal to capitulate to his injuries is admirable. I do know also that there is a deeper reason behind his remarkable recovery. Something that is driving him. And it is for that very same reason we are gathered here today."

Gagarin felt the strength of Testarov's gaze, and he looked across at the man, recognizing the fierce light that shone in his eyes. The bright, feverish light of an obsession that fueled Testarov's existence.

It was the need to track down and wipe out the team of American specialists responsible for the destruction of the Philippine operation.

Gagarin continued speaking.

"Over the past few years we have been plagued by the presence of an American-inspired team of specialists who have interfered with a number of our operations, and also those of people allied to our cause. This group has become widely feared and respected. And rightly so, because they are extremely good at what they do. Their track record is enviable. Over the years they have cost us men and money, not to mention a diminished credibility."

"I have heard of these so-called specialists," Kochak sneered. "They are nothing but a bunch of Yankee thugs. Probably drug addicts."

"No, Kochak," Testarov countered, "you couldn't be more wrong. Whatever else we feel about these men, one thing is certain. They are not thugs or drug addicts. On the contrary—they are resourceful, professional fighters of great courage. Let us never forget that. If we treat them casually, they will sweep us aside without hesitation."

"I can hardly believe what I am hearing," Kochak said. "One could almost say you are sympathetic toward the Americans."

Testarov turned toward him. Kochak was a fool. A brutal, unfeeling man with an arrogant attitude that did not allow him even the thought that there might be others his equal—or, heaven forbid, even better than he was. It was a bad mistake to make, especially where the team of American specialists was concerned, Testarov knew. Providing he lived long enough, Kochak just might learn the folly of underestimating the enemy.

"Kochak," Gagarin said in the tone of a tolerant parent chastising a child, "please try to curb your embarrassing tendency to bandy about meaningless words. We can't afford to do that. You have to remember we deal in hard—very hard—realities."

A red flush spread up Kochak's neck and face. He locked eyes with Testarov, and open hostility burned in his gaze. But he remained silent.

"As I was trying to explain," Gagarin continued, "we are here today in order to develop and put into operation a plan to rid us—once and for all—of the American team that has been causing so much trouble. A similar operation was mounted once before. It failed. I do not intend to travel that road again. Major Testarov, who has expressed personal interest in eliminating this group, will be in charge of the operation. Since he has had personal contact with the specialists and survived, he has knowledge of their abilities. For a time he even held one of them in captivity—a one-armed man named Katzenelenbogen. He appears to be the field commander. All information we have on this group will be at your disposal. Equipment and money will also be supplied, without question. We need this victory. If we can defeat this specialist group, we not only remove an embarrassment, but we also show that we are still a force to be reckoned with. And that is something we need to demonstrate during this unsettling time in Soviet history."

Gagarin turned to Testarov. "Leoni, do you accept this task?"

"Yes," Testarov said without a moment's hesitation.

He was fully aware of the implications. He was being offered a second chance. It was something rare in the KGB, where failure was a close relative of sudden death. If he didn't deliver this time, there would be no more chances. He would be buried so deep that no one would ever find him, and having an influential friend such as Gagarin would make no difference. Gagarin was putting himself on the line by sponsoring Testarov. Any forthcoming failure would endanger his position as well as that of anyone else involved.

"This dacha is at your disposal, Leoni. Use it to formulate your plan of operation. Pick yourself a team of men you can work with and trust. When you are ready, I will arrange accommodation for wherever you choose to locate your command center."

"Thank you, Colonel," Testarov said. He was still coming to terms with the notion that he had been offered a chance to redeem himself. Since his return to Russia, through his long recovery and the subsequent KGB inquiry, he had been wondering what his eventual fate would be. He had expected some dismal posting to a remote spot far away from civilization. Such thoughts had been on his mind during the drive from Moscow. He hadn't even entertained the thought that he might be offered a lifeline.

"Leoni," Gagarin said finally, "let me introduce someone who can offer unique information about our American specialists."

Testarov turned toward the third member of the group with keen interest. He had been curious about the man, but the unexpected turn of events had proved to be a distraction. Now Testarov watched as the man stood.

He was tall, with a supple, athletic build. Tanned, gray eyed, with light brown hair. He wore casual, well-cut clothing and he carried himself with easy confidence.

"This is Peter Reiger," Gagarin said. "He was born in the German Democratic Republic, but was recruited by the KGB during his teenage years and has been operating as a deep-cover operative for us in the Federal Republic. His most notable success was joining the Bundesgrenzschutz—the Federal Border Police—and three years ago being accepted as a member of the West German antiterrorist force, GSG-9. His association with these agencies has provided us with a great deal of useful information over the years. However, his peak was reached some months ago, when he was assigned to liase with a group of American specialists who were operating in

Germany. This group was seeking a terrorist organization that was targeting U.S. military personnel. Reiger not only worked with the group, but saw action with them and helped to eliminate the terrorists, who were neo-Nazis. It did us a favor. One thing we can certainly do without are fanatics, Nazis parading around Europe again.

"The American specialists, Leoni, were the same ones you came up against in the Philippines. Led by a one-armed man named Katzenelenbogen. So we now have two people with close-contact experience of this group. Put that combined experience to work in helping to identify and locate these men. And then wipe them out."

Testarov took the proffered hand and shook it enthusiastically, accepting Peter Reiger into his team.

1

Henry Talbot's final image was of the sun-bright Parisian boulevard with traffic honking and surging along the broad avenue. One moment his world was full of color and noise and the smells of Paris in the spring, and the next the universe exploded around him, briefly yet with a stunning ferocity that left him paralyzed in the scant seconds before oblivion took over. Death was the result of a burst of slugs from an AK-74 hitting the base of his skull and angling up through his brain to exit just above his eyebrows. He died without knowing who had killed him, or why.

Talbot was hurled to the ground, his limbs losing all control. He landed in a loose sprawl as blood from his shattered skull spilled across the sidewalk.

He didn't hear the screech of tires or see the black Mercedes-Benz sedan speed away from the scene. But others did, and were able to describe the car and its occupants. The very same car was found abandoned some hours later in a seedy Paris suburb, close to an entrance of the Paris subway.

The car was towed away to a police garage, where it was examined by members of the French antiterrorist squad. They had been called in on the case because it had all the earmarks of a terrorist assassination and Henry Talbot had been a member of the staff at the American Embassy in Paris. A minor member, yes, but still an American diplomat.

They found little in the car except a Russian cigarette wedged under a seat, and that in itself was nothing. But when this was added to the fact that a witness had thought he'd heard the gunman speak to the car driver in Russian, the French decided they had a lead, albeit extremely thin and heavy on speculation.

The information gleaned by the French eventually found its way, via official channels, to Washington, where it was analyzed and put on file.

Talbot was the third American to die over a period that was just a little under one month. The first had been a security officer at the American Embassy in Rome. He had been gunned down as he left his apartment one morning. His assailants had fled before the police appeared and the only clues to their identity were the shell casings from the weapon used in the brutal slaying. The casings were classified as 5.45 mm—which happened to be the caliber of the AK-74 on issue to the Soviet Armed Forces. The size and shape of the wound patterns verified the caliber of bullet used. The new 5.45 mm ammo was designed with a hollow tip to the steel-cored projectile. Such ammunition was generally used to gain maximum injury from the smaller caliber bullet. The hollowed tip deformed on impact with the target, causing the bullet to tumble, thus increasing the damage to the target. The same wound patterns were found on the body of the American translator working out of the U.S. Embassy in Oslo. The twenty-three-year-old woman from Maine had been ambushed while out driving, and had been shot in the face and chest as she'd sat behind the driving wheel.

Talbot's murder took place on a Tuesday morning, and on the Thursday of that week, another killing took place. This time it was in London.

It was just after 12.45 p.m. The British capital was basking in unusually warm weather for the time of year, and the streets were packed as offices and businesses were vacated for the lunch hour.

Harmon Walters, a tall, lanky American who originated from the Midwest, finished thumbing coins into the parking meter and made his way along Queens Gate in the general direction of the Royal Albert Hall. There was an upcoming concert in a week's time that Walters was determined to attend. As he'd had some time off from work, he had decided to use some of his time to book a couple of tickets for the concert. His current girlfriend had let slip that she would enjoy going to the performance, so Walters had figured it was time he did something different for her.

He wandered along the sunny street, taking his time. Walters never hurried. He saw no profit in racing around, missing all that was going on in the world. He much preferred to stroll from place to place, watching, admiring, listening.

As he passed Elvaston Place, a car eased out of the side road, turning left. It traveled slowly along the street, just behind him. Walters was not even aware of its presence.

The car suddenly accelerated and drew level with the American. The passenger window rolled down, and the muzzle of an AK-74 nosed into the open.

Harmon Walters's tranquil stroll ended in a bloody nightmare. The AK-74 erupted with noise, crackling autofire that drowned out all sound in the vicinity. The sustained blast of 5.45 mm slugs ripped into and through Walters's lean body, tearing flesh and organs alike. The American was tumbled across the sidewalk, spilling blood as he crashed to the ground. The merciless rain of bullets followed him, and it was only when the 30-round, orange-colored magazine of the AK-74 was empty that the gunfire ceased.

The driver of the murder car pulled away from the curb, merged quickly with the flowing traffic, then made a couple of quick turns that took him away from the scene of the slaughter. He plainly had a good working knowledge of London. Within a few minutes the car was heading toward Kensington and Hammersmith, then out in the direction of Ealing. By the time the police arrived on the scene, all traces of the killers and their car had vanished.

2

"What do you make of it all, Aaron?" Hal Brognola asked.

Aaron Kurtzman—popularly known as the Bear—activated his wheelchair, spinning away from his computer to face the Stony Man Fed. He held a printout in one massive fist, offering it to the man from the Justice Department.

Confined to a wheelchair after a bullet in the spine had taken away the use of his legs, Kurtzman spent every waking hour at his beloved computer banks, poring over the mass of information his machines pulled in.

Kurtzman could access computer systems that were denied the average user. If a system put up barriers, the Bear would find some way of overriding or bypassing them. The Stony Man communications and information-gathering section was second to none. Satellite links, through which the Stony Man operatives could call in using special number-codes fed through state-of-the-art scramblers, ensured fast contact with the base. There were occasions when information needed to be gained without delay. If official sanction was liable to take time, or be denied, Kurtzman would simply reach out and take the information he required.

He had been working for eight hours straight on a project Brognola had given him. The results were on the printout he handed to his chief.

"Give me the essentials," Brognola said.

"Over the last month there have been a number of violent deaths involving U.S. and allied personnel. The list of those killed includes Embassy staff, security people, some undercover agents. Nothing high-level. No link between the dead except that they were our people or they worked for us in some way."

"Indiscriminate killings?"

"Hard to say," Kurtzman replied. "I haven't established a definite pattern yet. But I'm still working on that angle."

"Take a break, fella," Brognola said.

"One thing I'm certain about," Kurtzman threw in. "It looks like the killings were the work of a hit team. A Soviet hit team."

"Why so sure?"

"From the various reports I've pulled in, there are similar points. The same weapon used each time. Russian AK-74, firing the 5.45 mm slug. Bullets taken from the victims all came from the same weapon. Witnesses have stated that they heard the killers talking in Russian. The orange-colored magazine of the AK-74 has also been described. The French antiterrorist squad found a Russian cigarette in a car that had been used in an attack in Paris. The cigarette was of a brand not available outside the Soviet Union."

Brognola frowned.

"Sounds a little too pat. Almost as if somebody wants us to believe the Soviets are involved. Maybe I'm getting too suspicious in my old age."

"Could be the Russians themselves," Kurtzman suggested. "Letting us know they aren't ready to roll over and play dead."

"I guess it could tie in with a rumor going around the circuit that a KGB strike force has been put together."

"Even though the Soviets are supposed to be easing off with the rough stuff?" Kurtzman queried.

"Mass media *glasnost*?" Brognola smiled. "I wish the real world would operate like that, Aaron. Trouble is, the espionage business doesn't work on a nine-to-five basis. National security is still the province of the backstage agencies, here and in Russia. Too many fingers in too many pies. Going to take a long time to work out who trusts who and why. Until then, we have to look after our own."

"At a guess I'd say this is one for Phoenix Force," the Bear suggested.

"Yeah," the Fed growled. "When I can get those overgrown Boy Scouts together." He attempted to sound like the heavy father, but his true feelings showed through.

"The President has already given his okay on the mission, so the sooner we can get the Force together, the sooner we can get this show on the road."

"Where are the guys?" Kurtzman asked.

"Taking some well-earned R&R," Brognola answered. "Wish I didn't have to break it up for them so soon, but that's the name of the game."

"I'll get myself some coffee, then get back on the keyboard," Kurtzman said. He picked up a telephone and punched out a number. "Hi, Barbara. I need something to keep me going. Strong coffee and one of your breakfasts. Bossman is with me, so make that two of everything. Give me a yell when it's ready."

"I'll have the calls put out for the team," Brognola said. "With a bit of luck we should have all the facts together by the time we get them on board."

3

A fine rain misted in from the Atlantic Ocean, catching Gary Manning in the open as he strolled along the quayside of St. Ives in Cornwall, situated on the southwest coast of Great Britain.

The Cornish fishing village, which now boasted a thriving tourist industry, still retained much of its historic charm. Narrow, cobbled streets, some rising steeply up the hills that surrounded the village, were practically deserted at this early time in the year. During the vacation season the village would play host to thousands, and the streets would be jammed solid. The two industries—fishing and tourism—existed side by side. An odd yet amicable partnership.

In the summer the Cornish weather attracted sunseekers, and St. Ives in particular also drew the surfers, who came to indulge in their sport along the beach at Porthmeor, where the Atlantic rollers provided them with the fast water they needed.

Manning had chosen to visit the area during the off-season because it offered peace and tranquility, and also provided a handy meeting place. The Canadian warrior, on a break from his activities with

Phoenix Force, had arranged to meet Karen Hoffe in St. Ives. The beautiful German girl, a member of the Frankfurt police department, had first met Manning during a Phoenix Force assignment in Germany. She had been working undercover, trying to find evidence against a man who turned out to be a member of the terrorist organization the Force was after. Karen had assisted Phoenix Force during its mission, and a mutual attraction had developed between her and Manning. They had continued their relationship since the mission, though their time together had been brief, due to the strictures of their respective professions. Luck seemed to be on their side, at present. Karen had been in London, attending a police convention, and had managed to combine the visit with some leave she had coming. The leave had coincided with Manning's spell of R&R from Phoenix Force, and the pair had decided to get away from people and lose themselves somewhere fairly isolated.

It had been a suggestion from David McCarter that had prompted Manning to book into a small hotel in St. Ives on his arrival in England. Karen's convention didn't finish until the following day, so Manning had traveled down to Cornwall in a rented car, phoned her from the hotel and left her directions.

After an early meal Manning had turned in, and woke refreshed the following morning. He had eaten breakfast, then decided to take a walk round St. Ives.

Karen wasn't scheduled to arrive until midafternoon.

The weather was mild, with a refreshing breeze coming in off the ocean. Manning had wandered around the town, allowing the atmosphere to wash over him and ease away the tension that had eaten into his very bones.

Recent missions with Phoenix Force had come thick and fast, giving the Stony Man warriors little time for relaxation. While they were involved in a mission there was no opportunity for easing the stress, for stepping back and taking a deep, cleansing breath. Phoenix Force played it straight down the line during mission time, channeling everything they had into the place and the time. The Force put personal feelings on the back burner during a mission, directing their energies toward defeating the opposition. When the mission was complete and they were on their own time, that was when the moment of truth was faced.

Manning had no doubts about his role with the Force. He was fully dedicated to the Stony Man doctrine. The need to combat evil in all its forms, as laid down by Mack Bolan, still held firm for the Canadian warrior. It was just a case of the flesh being prone to physical limitations despite the firm resolve of the mind. The hellgrounds took their toll, and the time came when the most selfless warrior needed to recharge his batteries. Gary Manning had need of some recharging, a time away from the noise and the stench of battle. This chance to be with Karen was exactly what the doctor would have ordered if he had been asked.

Manning's mind was empty of all thoughts, save those of the beautiful German girl. He had followed the street that led to the long quayside, content to simply walk. He wasn't even aware of the gray clouds rolling inland from the ocean until the first sheets of rain tumbled from the sky.

Over the next few minutes the rain increased, soaking the Canadian. He'd left the hotel without a coat, so he turned around and made his way back. By the time he reached the hotel, he was dripping wet. He entered, and while he was picking up his key from the small reception desk, he received an amused smile from the elderly clerk.

"Enjoying our bracing weather, Mr. Manning?"

"It's the reason I flew all the way from Canada," the Phoenix commando replied.

He took his key and made his way up to his room. Once inside, he peeled off his wet shirt and picked up a towel to dry himself.

That was when the telephone rang, and Manning eagerly picked up the receiver.

"Gary?" It was Karen's voice.

"Hi," he replied. "Hey, don't tell me. Let me guess. You've broken down? Run out of gas?"

"Please listen, Gary."

Manning sensed the urgency in her voice.

"Go ahead," he said.

"I believe there are people watching me," Karen explained.

"Odd choice of word," Manning pointed out. "Why 'watching'?"

"Deliberate," she replied. "I feel they are observing rather than following. As if they are waiting for me to do something."

"But what?" the Canadian asked, certain now that Karen was leading up to something.

"I'm not on any assignment at present," she said. "Nor am I involved in any important duty. So I must assume these people—whoever they might be—are waiting for me to make a move that will give them what they want."

"Sounds logical," Manning agreed.

"The only definite thing I'm about to do is meet you, Gary."

"Yeah, that's what just occurred to me."

The cold, hard suspicion clutched at Manning's gut. It was the possibility of its being true that caused the Phoenix warrior to feel uneasy.

An unspecified number of unknown people were using Karen to locate him.

Questions sprang into his mind.

Why were they looking for him? What did they want? And who were they?

"What do we do?" Karen asked.

"Where are you now?"

"In my room at the hotel. I was about to leave, but I decided to try and contact you first. Perhaps we should postpone our meeting, Gary."

"No," he said. "If there's something going on, we'll handle it now. No point putting it off."

"All right."

"Make your way down here just as we planned. We'll take it one step at a time. Don't do anything to make them feel they've been spotted. Once we're together, we'll draw them out."

"I'll see you later this afternoon," Karen said.

"Just take care."

4

By the middle of the day Hal Brognola had been in contact with every Phoenix Force member except Gary Manning.

Yakov Katzenelenbogen was heading in from New York, where he had been attending a seminar on human rights. The Israeli, who had firsthand experience of the subjects from his young days during the Second World War, still found there was much to be discussed about shortcomings worldwide.

From the South Side of Chicago, where he had been visiting relations, Calvin James responded to Brognola's call. The black Phoenix warrior, the team's youngest member, had been making a painful return to his hometown. It had been some time since he'd been back. James had decided it was time he visited the tough Chicago area where he had grown up. It reminded him just what he was fighting for when he went into combat with the Force. James had lost both mother and sister in the ghetto hell of the city, and he had been left with an anger that grew stronger as time went by. The ex-SEAL, who had served his country in Vietnam, had turned to crime fighting after the tragic deaths of his family, and had seen the invitation to join Phoenix Force as the only right and proper way to combat the scum of the world.

Rafael Encizo had a desire in his heart, too. It was the hope that one day he might return to his beloved Cuba, free from Castro's crippling dictatorship. His island home, now a depressed place of subdued people, was a gray shadow of its former self. The spirit of the land had been trampled underfoot by Castro in his obsession for Marxist perfection. All the blinkered leader had managed to do was to reduce Cuba to a debt-ridden nation that was living twenty years behind the times. Although Encizo wished Cuba free, he was not living in a dream. He knew that reality was far removed from wishful thinking. The Bay of Pigs had proved that. It was going to take more than a handful of patriots to liberate Cuba. That didn't stop the fiery Phoenix warrior from returning to Florida whenever he could in order to work among the Cubans who had fled to America. He worked with youth organizations, teaching young Cubans to scuba dive, giving them instruction in swimming and navigation. He had seen the need to give the lost youth of his country purpose, a path to walk that might lead them away from the lure of crime, drugs, easy money. Encizo knew, and accepted, that he could achieve little. But one teenager put on the path toward a decent life was worth all the effort. He was involved in such an exercise when the call came from Stony Man.

The first to arrive back at Stony Man was David McCarter. The brash, often insolent Briton, a Cockney from London's tough East End, had been relaxing not far from Washington. In true character, McCarter relaxed in a completely different way from everyone else. He had been at Langley Air Force Base, putting in some flying hours in the cockpit of a jet fighter. Hal Brognola had pulled some strings for permission to get the Briton access to the base and instruction from Air Force training staff.

He breezed into Stony Man like someone just back from a vacation in Hawaii.

"I bet I'm first." He grinned at Barbara Price as he wandered into the kitchen area.

Barbara glanced up from the pot of fresh coffee she was making. "Aren't you always?" she asked with a wry smile on her face.

McCarter peered into the cooler and pulled out a chilled can of Coke. He popped the tab and took a long swallow.

"Now I know I'm back," he smiled.

"Hal wants a word, soon as you get in."

"What have I done now? Used up all my luncheon vouchers again?"

"Why not go and see?"

The Briton nodded. "Good idea."

He ambled off and found Brognola in the War Room.

After a quick greeting, Brognola turned to the matter at hand. "David, do you know where Gary is?"

"Cornwall," McCarter replied. "You want me to get in touch?"

The Fed nodded. "Tell him he's wanted back here as soon as possible."

"Leave it to me, boss," the Cockney rebel said, and reached for the telephone.

5

Manning was seated in the hotel lounge beside a window that overlooked the small parking area. On a side table next to his chair, he had a pot of coffee and a plate with an assortment of sandwiches. He had been there for the past couple of hours, wanting to be on hand the moment Karen arrived.

It was still raining. The world was wrapped in a thin drizzle off the ocean, which pattered softly against the window.

A faint sound caught Manning's attention. He glanced around. It was the young waitress who had served him.

"Would you like some fresh coffee, sir?" she asked.

He shook his head. "This is fine."

She picked up the empty plate and retreated.

Then a car appeared at the head of the narrow street. It moved in the direction of the hotel and slowed as it neared. When it reached the parking area, it turned in and drew alongside Manning's own rented car.

Moments later Karen Hoffe stepped out.

The instant Manning recognized her, he got to his feet and snatched up the leather jacket on the chair next to his. He pulled it on as he walked from the hotel.

Karen saw him as he crossed the parking area. She smiled and held out her hands. "Hello," she said.

Manning held her, kissed her warmly, then turned her toward his car. He unlocked the door for her to get in, then went around to his side. Once behind the wheel, he started the engine and eased the rented Vauxhall Cavalier out of the parking area and onto the street. He rolled away from the hotel, sticking to narrow side streets, away from the town. He drove along a road that climbed steadily for a while, and the houses receded behind them. Suddenly they were in open countryside, and around them stretched the coarse moorland of the Cornish landscape. On their right, beyond the steep cliffs, lay the rolling swell of the rain-swept Atlantic. Manning put his foot down hard on the gas pedal to maintain their pace along the wet road.

"Were you followed?" he asked.

Karen nodded. Her eyes moved to look into the rearview mirror.

"A dark Rover sedan," she said. "It's behind us now."

"Are you armed at all?" Manning asked.

"No," Karen answered. "It wasn't possible to bring weapons into the country without a great deal of red tape. I saw no need at the time."

"Same here," Manning said. "It appears we were both wrong."

"I presume this drive into the country is for less than romantic reasons?" Karen asked.

Manning chuckled softly. "I hate to say it, but you're right."

"And I also presume you have a plan to deal with these people?"

In truth Manning's reply would have been negative. His intention had been to draw out Karen's pursuers and get them away from the town. If there was to be any kind of trouble, the Canadian didn't want innocent people involved. Too often, bystanders found themselves drawn into violent situations far beyond their worst nightmares. Manning had no intention of letting that happen. Both he and Karen were professionals. Being under threat was nothing new to either of them, and as professionals they were able to handle such occurrences. This time they had both been drawn into such a situation without the benefit of being armed. That was simply due to circumstances and had to be accepted. The difficulty would arise if their pursuers were armed.

Before Manning could reply to Karen's question, the trailing Rover accelerated. It roared up behind Manning's vehicle, then swerved out to pass it. As it drew level, Manning saw three men in the vehicle—two in the front and one in the rear seat. The Rover's driver began to drift in toward Manning's car.

"He wants to push us off the road," Karen gasped.

"Tough luck," the Canadian answered.

He yanked hard on the Vauxhall's wheel, sending the rental car smashing against the Rover. The other driver, obviously not expecting such a violent response, lost control momentarily. The Rover shot across the road, tires losing traction as the driver tried to regain control. Manning didn't give the guy the opportunity. He swung the Vauxhall at the Rover again, hitting hard. The Rover slithered, the front wheels striking the raised grass shoulder. It bounced over the edge of the road and plunged into the thick bracken. It plowed on a few more yards, then came to a shuddering halt.

Manning had already braked the Vauxhall, yanking the gearshift into reverse. He floored the gas pedal, steering the car back along the road. He brought it to a halt, kicking open his door. Plunging off the road, the agile Canadian ran in the direction of the stalled Rover.

He reached it as the front-seat passenger began to open his door. Manning caught a glimpse of an autopistol in the guy's hand. It was an FN-35DA, 9 mm with a 14-shot magazine, made by the Fabrique Nationale company of Belgium. The man was struggling to get his balance when Manning yanked open the door, caught hold of his collar and hauled him out of the Rover. Yelling in what sounded like Russian, the man lashed out at Manning with the FN-35DA autopistol. The Phoenix pro ducked under the blow, then countered with a hard right that connected with his opponent's jaw. The gunman's head

jerked back, and blood oozed on his heavy chin.
Manning slammed his foot against the door, driving
it into contact with the gunman's arm. The man
roared with agony as the bone snapped, and the pistol dropped from his fingers. Manning caught it before it touched the ground.

Out of the corner of his eye he spotted the rear
passenger emerging from his door. The man held an
Ingram MAC-10 in his hands. He raised it above the
level of the door frame and triggered the weapon. A
stream of 9 mm slugs chewed into the glass and steel
of the front door, but Manning had already dropped
to his knees. He felt shattered glass falling across his
back. He reacted instinctively, thrusting the muzzle
of the FN-35DA he'd acquired in the direction of the
rear door. He pulled the trigger, feeling the heavy
autopistol kick back as it fired.

Manning's shot passed through the glass of the
rear door and punched into the subgunner's chest.
He slumped back against the door frame. His dark-
featured face twisted in agony as the bullet did its
damage. Despite his injury, he attempted to reline the
Ingram on Manning again, struggling to bring the
muzzle down.

No more than a few seconds had elapsed since
Manning had fired. His finger was already easing
back on the trigger as the wounded subgunner tried
to pull his weapon back on target. The Phoenix
fighter continued the movement, the autopistol
snapping out its second shot, sending a slug crashing into the chest—this time directly over the heart.

The fatally wounded man folded and slipped across the rear seat of the Rover.

Manning heard Karen's shouted warning and half turned in the direction of the driver's side of the car. He caught a hurried glimpse of the driver's face across the Rover's roof. Angry eyes, behind the sights of an autopistol, met Manning's. The Canadian shoved himself away from the car, seeking the cover of the ground. He heard the crack of a shot and felt the rush of the bullet passing overhead.

He hit the sodden ground and rolled away from the bulk of the Rover, conscious of the presence of the armed driver. Coming to a stop, the Phoenix commando peered beneath the vehicle and spotted the driver's legs as the man edged toward the front of the Rover.

Manning pushed himself up off the ground, keeping low and extending the hand carrying the autopistol.

The driver's head and shoulders came into view, his own pistol held up and ready.

Both weapons fired in the same instant.

Manning gasped as a bullet grazed his left shoulder. The sudden pain made him snatch at the FN-35DA's trigger again and yet again, the heavy weapon thundering loudly.

The extra shots were superfluous. Manning's first slug had caught the driver just below the right eye. The force of the shot yanked the man's head round, presenting a broader, side-on target for the second and third shots. The driver was thrust away from the front of the car, his face and skull abruptly misshapen. He crashed to the ground in a twitching sprawl.

Manning turned the gun in the direction of the first man who had emerged from the Rover. That opponent was on his knees, gripping his broken arm, while he let his head hang morosely.

Reaching out, Manning raised the man's head and stared into the cold eyes that fixed on him.

"You understand English?" he asked.

"I understand," the man replied. His voice was heavily accented, and there was no mistaking where he was from.

"Russian," Karen said. She had come up behind Manning.

"What did you want with us?" the Canadian warrior asked.

The Russian shrugged. "I don't have to tell you anything."

"That's true," Manning replied. He glanced at Karen. "Pick up any weapons you can find. Search the car and the bodies for clues of any kind."

Karen nodded and moved to carry out the task.

"What happens to me?" the Russian asked.

"Not my concern," Manning told him, standing up. "You set the rules of the game, pal. Now you have to play by them."

"What does this mean?" demanded the angry Soviet.

"It means you're on your own."

Karen returned shortly. She had piled the weapons collected from the dead men.

"The car is clean," she said. "Nothing. Not even a gum wrapper."

"Let's get the hell away from here," Manning said, and turned to the Vauxhall.

Manning started the car and turned it around, heading back in the direction of St. Ives. For a while neither he nor Karen spoke. They allowed themselves to relax, to come to terms with the sudden explosion of violence.

"I'm sorry for the trouble I brought you," the German woman said.

"Hey, you can quit that kind of talk," Manning told her. "I'm just glad you didn't get hurt."

"Oh, Gary," Karen exclaimed. "What about your shoulder?"

He became aware of the slight tingling sensation where the bullet had clipped him.

"I'm fine. But damned angry."

"Why?"

"Because I can't figure out who wants me dead. Or how they knew we were going to meet."

"I told no one, as we agreed earlier."

"If that's the case, then who do we know who knows about our relationship?"

"Only the others who were with you in Germany."

Manning nodded. "Yeah. That's the part that worries me."

6

"Sorry about breaking into your R&R, fellas," Brognola said apologetically. He dropped the stack of folders he was carrying on the large table and gazed around the War Room.

McCarter was there. So were Katz, James and Encizo. Only Gary Manning was still absent.

"This must be urgent, Hal," Katz said, glancing up from lighting a cigarette.

The Fed nodded. "It's also a puzzler," he threw in as he sat down.

Encizo, standing beside the bubbling coffee percolator, looked over his shoulder.

"So urgent we can't wait for Gary to arrive?"

"Yeah," Brognola said. "He'll catch up with you guys at your destination."

"Where will that be?" James asked impatiently. He was still recovering from his frantic journey from Chicago.

McCarter shook his head in disapproval. "I think someone got out of the wrong side of the bed."

"Lay off, McCarter," James snapped.

"Let us all just relax," Katz said gently. "We've had a long, tiring day. Why don't we just listen to what Hal has to say? Go ahead, Hal."

"There has been a series of murders over the last few weeks. The majority of the victims have been U.S. citizens. And though there have also been some non-Americans killed, they were people working for the U.S. in one form or another. Mostly in the security business. Information gatherers. Spotters. Local liaison agents. The U.S. citizens were mainly Embassy personnel. We've run all the information through the computers but can't come up with any logical pattern. They appear to be random acts of violence. Without reason. Killing for killing's sake."

"Any idea who might be responsible?" Katz asked.

"Maybe," Brognola replied. "We have two points of reference. There has been a rumor about a KGB hit team being on the loose for a while now. Nothing concrete, just scraps coming in from Intelligence sources. Secondly we have some bits of information or physical evidence following local investigation. The bottom line reads, Russians involved. Use of Soviet weapons. Small items like a Russian brand of cigarette found in one of the hit cars. Witnesses identifying Russian as the language being used by the killers."

"Sounds like a sloppy bunch to me," McCarter said.

"If they're Soviet," Encizo remarked, "they must be the reserve team."

"That was the point that bugged me," Brognola admitted. "The Russians are usually hot on efficiency. The KGB tends to be almost fanatical about it."

"Maybe they want to be noticed," Encizo suggested.

"The last thing a hit team wants is publicity," James said, "and especially a KGB team. Those guys thrive on playing the invisible man."

"So what's the game?" Katz asked. "There's something we're missing here. Come on, you guys, pin it down."

"Could be an invitation," McCarter said.

"To what? A goddamned square dance?" James snapped.

"Maybe it's the KGB's way of saying come out and fight, Phoenix Force. Showdown time. High noon and all that."

"What is he rambling about?" James asked.

"Are you suggesting this is nothing more than a charade? A deliberate come-on?" Katz asked. "That all this activity is aimed at us?"

"Jesus, can't you see?" McCarter scoffed. "We've hacked the KGB up more than once. Spoiled any number of their dirty schemes over the last few years. Cost them a lot in men and money and done their image a lot of harm. They'd give a year's pay to wipe us out. What better way to attract our attention then by murdering a few American citizens and letting us know who did it?"

Silence descended over the War Room as McCarter's words were absorbed and considered.

"I'll let you guys decide the merits of David's suggestion," Brognola said finally. "For what it's worth, we've had a readout from one of the Pentagon think tanks. They've been doing some in-depth analysis on the Russian peace initiative. One of their evaluations does suggest that there might be some resistance by dyed-in-the-wool Marxists. Those who don't want to change the status quo. The KGB isn't going to roll over and play cute without a fight. It's going to be a hell of a job getting them to loosen their grip on the national throat. It would be like asking the CIA to pack up and go home. People with power don't relish letting go. And our Russian friends have had power and control all their own way for a long time."

"Are you saying that David's theory could have some merit?" Calvin James inquired. "That they could be trying to take us out to show they can still cut it?"

Brognola shrugged. "Wouldn't do them any harm. Would it?"

"I guess not," James conceded.

"It's something to keep in mind," Katz remarked.

"In the meantime," Brognola said, opening one of his folders, "we do have something for you to get your collective teeth into."

"Another clue?" McCarter asked eagerly.

"Don't push your luck, David," Katz warned sternly.

"Just before you guys checked in, we had a report from one of our sources in Marseilles. Our guy down there has bought some information that fits the ID of this KGB squad. They were spotted in town two days ago and were reported to be still around."

"Marseilles?" Katz mused. "Why there?"

"There was a hint they might be meeting up with some representatives from Libya."

"Not Khaddafi's crazies again," Rafael Encizo said. "Team the KGB up with those bastards, and we could have real trouble."

"Not if we can get to them in time to stop any deal they might be making," Katz pointed out.

"There's a plane ready to fly you out," Brognola said. "Gary will meet you in Marseilles."

"And?" Katz asked.

Brognola glanced at him. "You expecting more?"

The Israeli calmly nodded, and the Fed smiled. He'd clearly known he wouldn't get off so quickly.

"Gary ran into some trouble while he was in England. He handled it. I'm not sure, but it might— *only might*—have some connection with the mission."

"More mystery," McCarter muttered as he stood up.

"How do we stand on taking weapons into France?" Calvin James asked.

"At the moment, we don't," Brognola admitted. "You'll have to tread carefully on this. We're trying to get some cooperation from the French authorities. Until we do, you'll have to play it by ear. Our man in Marseilles will be able to fix you up with some items. Just keep in mind that the French have a reputation for being tough on anyone who contravenes their regulations.''

''Yeah?'' James snapped. ''When I think about those Americans who've been wasted, I start feeling pretty damned tough myself. French or no French, if I meet the guys responsible, it's gonna be ass-kicking time.''

''You know, Hal,'' McCarter said in a high-toned British accent, ''I'm inclined to agree with my chum from the South Side of old Chicago. He isn't very often right, but this time he's hit the nail on the top of its jolly old head.''

''If I translate that right, my man, I do believe you've just agreed with me,'' James replied.

The Cockney grinned at the black warrior. ''Shall we go?'' he asked.

7

Gary Manning linked up with his four fellow Phoenix Force teammates at Marignane Airport, which lay seventeen miles northwest of the city of Marseilles. The Canadian had rented a large Citroën sedan. Once the Force's luggage had been stowed in the trunk, everyone climbed into the French automobile. Katz sat next to Manning. The others took the wide rear seat, with McCarter lounging between James and Encizo.

Heading east from the airport, Manning picked up the A7 highway going south. It was a fast route that would take them directly to Marseilles and the hotel into which they had been booked.

It was midafternoon. The day was warm without being uncomfortable, as it was too early in the year for the weather to have peaked. Even so, the climate was extremely agreeable.

Off to the right the land gave way to the blue waters of the Mediterranean. Above, the sky maintained its shimmering perfection, with only a few scattered white clouds showing.

Katz gave Manning a concise briefing about the mission—adding that for the time being, they needed to move with caution—hoping that the home team would quickly get them clearance from the French authorities.

"So at the moment we're unsanctioned?"

Katz nodded, and Manning gripped the steering wheel in unconcealed frustration. "That doesn't exactly help the situation," he said.

"Believe me, Gary," Katz said soothingly, "I don't like the idea myself. But we had to move fast. Too much delay might have lost us our opportunity for making contact with this Soviet team."

"Without weapons?"

"Our contact man should be arranging to put that right," the Israeli said.

"Let's hope he backs his talk with action," James remarked.

McCarter felt it was time he had his say on the matter. "Hey, cheer up. This won't be the first time we've had to operate without permission. And we'll get weapons, no problem there."

"He treats every situation like a damned vacation," James muttered.

"For him every mission *is* a vacation," Encizo pointed out.

"Look, you can't fault me because I enjoy my work," the Cockney complained.

"Hal told me you encountered a problem while you were in England," Katz said to Manning. "You want to fill me in?"

Manning related the entire episode, starting from Karen's telephone call and concluding with the confrontation with the armed men.

"Now *that* is what I call a fun-filled break," McCarter chimed in breezily.

The annoyed stares he received from the rest of the Force convinced the Briton that it was time for a silent withdrawal.

"How did you leave things over there?" Katz asked.

"When we got back to the hotel," the Canadian explained, "there was a message from David. Incorporated into it was the code word telling me to call Stony Man. I did and spoke to Hal. Laid it on the line what had happened. He told me to check out of the hotel and head straight for Heathrow. He said there would be someone there to meet me. This contact would have instructions for me. A cleanup squad would handle things in Cornwall. So that was exactly what we did. At Heathrow the contact met me with tickets and all the necessary documentation to get us into France. As soon as we arrived, I hired this car and we booked in, then waited for you guys."

"You keep saying 'we,' Gary," Katz interrupted. "Are you saying that Karen is here in Marseilles?"

"How should I have handled it, Yakov? Left her on her own? No telling if these people might try again or perhaps use her as a direct way of getting at me."

"We are on a mission," the Phoenix commander pointed out.

Manning's face darkened with anger. "Just say the word, Yakov, and I'll withdraw. If you believe what I've done puts the mission in jeopardy, I'm out. There's no way I'd do anything to put you at risk— any of you. But I can't just walk away if Karen is in danger."

"I'm not saying you've harmed the mission," Katz stated. "All I meant to suggest was the risk that Karen presents. Her being around may cloud your judgment. You know we can't afford any distractions in an operational situation."

"What are you expecting me to do?" Manning asked. "Ask for a break in the middle of a firefight so I can jump into bed with her?"

"No," Katz said. "Now you're overreacting, the same as I did a minute ago."

"I believe Gary did the only thing he could have under the circumstances," Encizo said.

"Yeah," James agreed. "He was on the spot, Katz. Caught between a rock and a hard place. Only thing you can do then is follow your instinct."

"I see," Katz remarked. "Ganging up on me."

"What about my opinion?" McCarter asked. "Nobody want to know what I think?"

The silence that followed was meaningful. "Okay," the Briton said. "I can take a hint."

"Gary, I'm not trying to come down with a heavy hand," Katz explained. "I can understand you wanting to protect Karen. But I was concerned about her safety if she was in close proximity to the Force if we got into a combat situation. It would be tragic if her being near us for protection placed her life in danger."

Manning quickly nodded in understanding. "I explained that to her, Katz, and she accepts it. Don't forget that she is a professional law officer, trained to deal with difficult situations. And don't forget how she handled being with us during our mission in Germany."

"That's true," Katz admitted. "She might be able to throw some light on the people who tracked you in England."

"We've already gone over that. Neither of us could come up with anything. The problem is, Katz, that we're the only ones who know about my connection with Karen. If you recall, after the German mission we kept our relationship strictly under wraps. Karen didn't say anything to her people. I'm certain of that. So who else knew?"

"Someone has made a connection," Encizo stated. "Definite enough to be able to use Karen to lead them to you."

"Don't remind me," the Canadian said. "It's bugging me not to be able to put a face to that connection."

"When we get settled in the hotel, I'll put through a call to the Bear," Katz said. "Get him to run a check on everyone concerned with the German mission who might have had knowledge about Karen's involvement with us. It's a long shot, but it might lead to something. In the meantime, we can all do some thinking on the subject. See if we get lucky."

"Am I included in this little project?" McCarter asked.

"Why should you be different than anyone else?" Katz asked. "I'm all for you doing some thinking. It means you won't be doing as much talking as you usually do."

"What does that mean?" the Cockney demanded.

James was grinning widely as he said, "I guess what he's trying to say diplomatically is that you can't think and talk at the same time."

"You know I should be upset at a remark like that."

Encizo glanced at the Briton. "So why aren't you?"

"Because I think he could be right," McCarter answered.

Shortly they were rolling into Marseilles. The Citroën sped along the highway that followed the four-mile stretch of the docks, bringing them eventually to the Vieux Port—the Old Port. Turning onto Boulevard Charles Livon, Manning drove to the Sofitel Vieux Port, the hotel into which Phoenix Force had been booked.

The Sofitel was one of the city's more modern hotels and boasted soundproofing of its air-conditioned rooms, as well as two restaurants, one of which, the Trois Forts, was acclaimed as one of the best in Marseilles.

Manning parked the car. The Force took their luggage from the trunk and made their way inside the hotel. Manning led the way to the reception desk, where he introduced the Force as the rest of his party. The team's cover for this particular mission was that they were a group of businessmen interested in investing hard cash in a leisure complex along the coast just outside Marseilles. There actually was such a proposed site, and the owners were looking for foreign investment. After registering, the Force made their way up to their individual rooms, where they took time to freshen up after the long flight. When they were ready, they made their way to Katz's room for a briefing session.

McCarter and James were the first to appear. When Katz let them into the room, the Briton caught his attention.

"Something wrong?" the Israeli asked.

"How long before this contact man shows? I don't like wandering around without something to defend myself."

"I remember an article years ago," James said. "It described how you could kill a man with a rolled-up magazine."

"I'll try to bear that in mind next time some mug tries to blow me apart with a bloody AK-47," McCarter grouched. "Wasn't that article written by the same joker who smashed concrete blocks with his head? The guy was a nut case."

"To answer your question, David," Katz began, "Frank Delgado, our contact man, should be joining us any time now. He had to complete arrangements first. Hopefully he will be able to supply us with some kind of weaponry."

"Oh, great," the impatient Cockney said. "Maybe I'll get the bow and arrow."

"I don't think it will be that bad." Katz smiled.

"Well, if he doesn't come up with decent weapons, I'll make my own arrangements."

"What are you going to do? Raid the local police station?" James asked. "Or do you have friends in town?"

"A friend," McCarter answered. "But a damned good one. He runs a small boat-charter company along with his French partner."

"Your friend—is he British?" Katz asked.

"Irish," McCarter said. "Completely crazy and fighting mad."

"Does sound like one of your friends," James murmured.

Just then there was a tap on the door, and Manning and Encizo were admitted into the room. They joined the others, then Manning turning to speak to Katz.

"Karen knows we have things to discuss. She'll join us later."

"Good," Katz said.

The Phoenix warriors settled themselves in various places around the room and waited for Katz to open the conversation.

"We have two objectives," he said. "Locate and put out of action this so-called elite team of KGB operatives. We need to gain some information on them so we can assess the potential of the threat they offer. And also to find out whether they are actually seeking some kind of confrontation with us.

"Secondly we need to know who pointed the finger at Karen and used her to lead them to Gary. Are they tied in with the KGB squad or not?"

"Don't forget the Libyans," Encizo reminded him.

"I haven't," Katz replied. "We check that out, as well. It may be nothing but a blind. On the other hand, it could be some KGB mischief being set up."

"Do we split up?" Encizo asked. "We can cover more ground that way."

Katz looked slowly around. "For a while. You want to team up with David, Rafael? You might be able to keep him from doing something rash."

The Cuban made an easy gesture and cast a quick smile at the Briton.

"I'd like to check out this information. The one who fed the story about the Soviets to Delgado. See if you can make a judgment on his dependability."

"It's done," McCarter said.

A knock on the door drew everyone's attention. Katz crossed to the door. "Who is it?"

"Frank Delgado."

Katz opened the door and let the contact man in.

Delgado was a dark-haired Mediterranean type. He was stocky and had a swarthy complexion, with the hair brushed sleekly back from his forehead. He wore a lightweight tan suit. An attaché case was tucked under his right arm.

Manning made the introductions, identifying each man by his cover name.

"I hope these will do," Delgado said as he placed the attaché case on the bed and opened it. Inside lay five Walther P-88 double-action autopistols. Made to fire 9 mm parabellum rounds, the P-88 held 15 rounds in its magazine. The pistol's design incorporated an internal safety, which only allowed firing if the trigger was pulled all the way through. The autopistol was comfortable to handle and was well balanced. Included with the weapons were extra magazines and four boxes of ammunition.

Manning picked up one of the pistols, weighing it in his hand. "Excellent," he commented. "I won't ask you where you got them, but I couldn't have done better myself in such a short time."

"Pretty fair," McCarter muttered. He worked the P-88's action. "Pity you couldn't have picked up some subguns, as well."

"These will do fine, Delgado," Katz said.

"Is there anything else you need, apart from weapons?" Delgado asked. "I was instructed by Washington to give you every assistance I can. It was also made clear to me that you have total control over this assignment."

"Yes," Katz said. "Sorry about that. Our way of operating demands that we act as we see fit, without consultation. It would cramp our style having to get clearance before we made a move."

Delgado rubbed his unshaven chin. "I guess you know your own business. So, do you need anything?"

"A good meal and some sleep wouldn't go amiss," Manning said.

"Later," Katz told the Canadian, then turned back to Delgado. "What about the information on our Russian friends?"

"Came to me via an informant named Ferney," Delgado explained. "He's been around Marseilles for years. He's a greasy son of a bitch, but he trades good information. I've dealt with him a few times, and he's always come up with the goods. I've never trusted him fully, though. Something about the man that makes me keep my back to the wall when I'm talking to him. You know what I mean?"

McCarter nodded. "We've come across his kind before."

"Ferney came to me with information about a KGB squad in the area. There's a fair amount of espionage trade in this vicinity, what with Marseilles being located where it is. Spain on one side. Italy on the other. North Africa across the Med to the south. Add the fact that Marseilles is still a busy port, handling ships from all over the world, which means there is a lot of unofficial comings and goings. So I wasn't surprised to hear the Russians were in town, and according to Ferney, they had something going with a group of Libyans. What that is, I haven't been able to find out. Ferney's description of the KGB team fitted the profile we've managed to put together. So I kicked the information back to Washington and waited to hear their response.''

"And ended up with us," James said.

Delgado smiled. ''No sweat there. I'm just a spotter. I gather information and assess it, then push it off to HQ. If they figure it's worth following up, they assign a field operative and he takes over. That's as far as I go.''

"Doesn't it get boring?'' Encizo asked.

Delgado shrugged. ''Not for me. I'm no action man. Never have been. Hell, I'm happy enough doing what I do. At least I'm seeing the world. And Marseilles is a hell of a town.''

"Is it still as tough as I remember it?'' McCarter asked.

"If you go to the right places,'' Delgado answered. ''North of La Canebière on the Rue Thubaneau—now there is a rough area. They'll slit your throat down there just for the fun of it.''

"Hasn't changed much.'' McCarter grinned.

"Maybe I forgot to mention that our friend Ferney lives out on Rue Thubaneau,'' Delgado added.

"Great,'' Encizo remarked. ''Trust me to fall for the dirty detail.''

"Don't forget you're with me,'' McCarter pointed out to the Cuban.

Encizo glanced at him. ''I was *trying* to forget that.''

8

"What is happening?" Leoni Testarov asked as Peter Reiger entered the room.

The East German crossed to the window and stared out across the walled garden of the villa. It was perched on a hill overlooking the city, giving a broad view of the bay and the Mediterranean.

"I like the climate here," Reiger said. "It's very pleasant, don't you think?"

"Yes, I agree. And the wine is also pleasant. But what has this to do with our business, Peter?"

Reiger turned to glance at the Russian, and a faintly mocking smile was on his lips. "I am aware of the importance of our mission, Leoni, and I will not be distracted. On the other hand, a few moments admiring the view won't do any harm."

Testarov eased himself out of the lounger and joined Reiger at the open window. He had to admit that the scenery was impressive. The countryside surrounding Marseilles was striking, as was the bustling city itself. Testarov had been glad to move to the comparative calm of the villa, away from the confines of the metropolis. It was a place where he could sit back and think, to plan, to deliberate on future moves.

Also there were the Libyans to consider. Testarov's instructions had been clear. He was to give whatever aid he could to the Libyans. It would show good faith. It bought markers that could prove profitable in the future. The Middle East was still an unsettled place, with shifting demarcation lines and many players seeking sides. Khaddafi, for all his faults, ruled a country that owned rich oil fields. Keeping the peace with the mad colonel was worth the effort. In any area like the Middle East, the volatile political and military situations were fair game for those seeking an advantage. Long-term strategy dictated the vital demand to maintain relations with those who controlled the oil fields. So playing big brother to Khaddafi would help keep the U.S.S.R.'s options open.

As far as Testarov was concerned, the presence of the Libyans posed a security problem. He could keep control of his own people, but not the Arabs. Their leader, known only as Rashid, was a tense, single-minded individual who lived and breathed his religion as if he was a stand-in for Allah himself. He possessed tunnel vision; nothing existed save his mission, and nothing else mattered. The most important event in global history, at least for Rashid, was the execution of his holy crusade against the United States. Rashid was a pain in the ass, but orders were orders, so Testarov had to grit his teeth and bear it.

"So, Peter, we have taken in the pastoral delights of Marseilles and its environs," Testarov said after a while. "Can I repeat my question?"

"No need," Reiger replied. "I can tell you now that our friends have arrived. They were picked up at Marignane Airport and driven into Marseilles by the Canadian. They went directly to their hotel, and according to our people, they are still inside. They were joined recently by the American, Delgado."

Testarov absorbed the information quietly, but he was smiling inwardly. The American team had taken the bait and followed it to Marseilles. The gradually leaked snippets of information about the KGB strike force, plus the deliberate killings of American citizens and employees, had attracted the attention of the U.S. administration. Full of indignation at the wanton slaughter of their people, the Americans had sent out the specialist team to avenge the dead. The final strand in Testarov's web had been the orchestrated leakage of information via the man named Ferney. The Frenchman was nothing more than a peddler of information. He believed he was clever and a skilled negotiator, but Testarov had found him to be a man of little intellect and less morals. When Testarov had woven his tale of intrigue, larded heavily with money, Ferney had accepted it without a moment's hesitation. The tale was delivered to the local American agent, who in turn passed it to his superiors in Washington.

Although that part of his plan appeared to be working out, Testarov was less than satisfied with the result of Kochak's earlier attempt at removing a member of the American team. Reiger had given them a lead—a German policewoman who had become involved with one of the specialists during their foray in Germany. Reiger had discovered that the woman was to travel to England to attend a police convention in London. Around that time the man she was involved with turned up in England. It was decided to follow the woman discreetly in case she had made arrangements to meet the man. It all worked out fine until the men assigned to the task, who were under Kochak's direct control as section chief, received an order to move in and eliminate the man.

By the time Testarov found out, it was too late. Kochak's team had made their move and had been taken out by the lone specialist. What should have been routine surveillance became a near massacre, with two men dead and a third wounded. Testarov had been furious and had rounded on Kochak with a blistering attack about his incompetence and utter stupidity. Kochak had defended himself by insisting that he had been acting in the interests of the strike force. His contention was that it would have reduced the odds if one of the specialists was removed. He was simply doing his job. No amount of recrimination altered Kochak's stance. The man had figured he was right, and there was no swaying him from that decision.

Testarov had known from the start that he was going to have to accept the result of Kochak's error in judgment. It took a great deal of willpower. In the end Testarov did accept the defeat, though it left him with a sour taste in his mouth. Brooding about it would change nothing, he realized, and carried on with the operation. At any rate, the target was now within Testarov's sight.

"What do we do next?" Reiger asked.

"Let us sit back and watch what *they* do," Testarov suggested. "We may get lucky and have one of them fall into our hands." The KGB man held up a hand as Reiger glanced at him. "I know exactly what you are thinking, Peter, and you would be correct. I am also recalling that I had one of them in my hands during the Philippine farce, and I lost him that time. It does not necessarily follow that I would repeat the error if I managed to catch one of them again. Now does it?"

Reiger shook his head. "No, it does not," he said. "I should not have allowed myself to fall prey to such thoughts."

"Human nature is such that it makes us ask these questions, Peter. I would have done the same if our positions had been reversed."

"How long do we wait before we do anything?"

"Knowing our American friends, I am sure they will soon be in action. My experience of them reminds me that they are resourceful and always eager to be on the move."

"I can vouch for that. During my time with them, we crossed half of Germany in record time."

Behind Testarov a telephone rang. He turned to pick it up and listened intently before uttering a few words. He replaced the receiver and caught Reiger's eye.

"It seems our American friends are even more restless than usual. Two of them have left the hotel and are making their way into Marseilles. Our people are following them. Perhaps we will have a result sooner than we expected. I hoped they might split up. This could give us a better chance to either capture or eliminate some of them."

"If two have gone off on their own, might this not be an opportune time to move against the others?" Reiger asked. "Send some of our men to the hotel?"

"Tempting," Testarov agreed. "But I think we would be wiser to wait until we have them on less public ground. I would prefer to get them somewhere isolated. Too many things can work against you in a hotel. There are people in the vicinity we cannot have control over. It's impossible to predict what they might do."

"Then why don't we lure the rest out? Create a situation to draw them from the hotel. Bring them to a place we choose and then eliminate them?"

"Yes, such a plan has merit," Testarov allowed. "Let us start making preparations. In the meantime, we will observe and see where this other pair ends up."

9

From the moment of its founding in 600 B.C.—by
Greeks from Phocea—Marseilles has had a check-
ered past. In its early years the port played a part in
Roman history, though not always to its benefit.
During the Crusades its appetite for commerce
brought great prosperity, and it was on this that
Marseilles—the oldest town in France—built its reputation. The country's foremost port saw travelers
from every point of the compass. Much of the Old
Port of Marseilles was destroyed by the Germans
during the Second World War, and the present-day
docks are stark, modern constructions. But Marseilles has managed to retain its character: it has always been a rowdy, boisterous city, a place of vivid
contrasts. It has a reputation for being a tough town,
with a gangster fraternity based on Mafia lines, and
there are places that visitors are advised to stay away
from, especially at night.

The Rue Thubaneau was one of those places.
During daylight hours the cracks showed, revealing
the downright squalor of the place, where prosti-
tutes and pimps plied their trade. At night the garish

illumination only succeeded in emphasizing the sorry atmosphere.

The cab dropped McCarter and Encizo at the edge of the neighborhood. The moment the driver was paid, he floored the gas pedal and took off, leaving the Phoenix pair to their fate. The cab's taillights winked red as the vehicle vanished into the early-evening gloom.

"The way that guy took off doesn't exactly fill me with confidence," Encizo muttered, feeling under his coat for the butt of the Walther P-88 tucked in his waistband.

"Look, you're safe enough with me," McCarter grinned, looking wolfish under the glare of a street lamp.

Encizo glanced along the street. Crowds were thronging on the sidewalks, moving in and out of the bars and the dubious-looking clubs. Neon lights advertised various entertainments, and the shills were out in force, doing their best to entice potential customers in off the street.

"This Ferney must be a masochist to want to live in a place like this," he said.

"Takes all sorts, chum," McCarter replied. "Come on, let's go and knock him up."

He led the way into the crowd, striding forward with his usual confidence.

They hadn't gone far before the hard sell started. Pimps, shills and even the ladies of the night made their presence known. Each vying with the others for the chance at a business deal or an easy way to part the customer from his money.

None of them got very far. McCarter had the ability to switch from casual charm to cold enmity in an instant, and all it took was one look into those bleak eyes to silence the hardest street dealer. Encizo's powerful appearance had a similar effect, keeping at bay even the most persistent.

Delgado's directions had been specific and took the Phoenix warriors to the dismal side street that led off the main drag. Even McCarter paused before he turned into the dank, grubby cul-de-sac. "I know rats from the East End who wouldn't walk down this alley," he muttered.

"This is what you call a *mean* street," Encizo observed.

McCarter loosened his sports coat. "Along the yellow brick road," he said.

There was little light ahead of them. Street lamps had not yet reached this part of Marseilles. Shadows lay in wait like black holes. As McCarter and Encizo walked along the uneven sidewalk, a figure stepped into view. Even there, on a dead-end street, the women of the night hovered in the doorways.

"Shove off," McCarter snapped ungraciously, and though she might not have understood the language, the woman caught the hostility in the Briton's tone. She melted back into the darkness as McCarter strode on by, his mind in gear now for what lay ahead.

"Over there," Encizo said, pointing to a four-story house, one of a row of terraced buildings.

The number over the entrance established it as the building Delgado had detailed.

"Can't say it's an inviting-looking building," McCarter muttered.

"I hate to go in myself, but I don't think Ferney will come down to us," Encizo commented. "Hey, think of it as an experience, David. How the other half lives."

"That knowledge I can live happily without."

They entered the building. The entrance hall was shabby, with stale air heavy with dust and the odors of overcooked food. A grubby bulb hung from a frayed cord, casting pale, cold light over the stained walls and uncarpeted floor.

"Two floors up," Encizo said, and they climbed the creaking stairs.

Reaching the floor they wanted, the Stony Man warriors moved along it until they got to the door they were looking for. Without hesitating, Encizo rapped on the panel. The sound of sudden movement inside the room told them that someone was at home. Encizo knocked again.

An angry voice shouted in rapid French, the words tumbling over one another.

"Ferney?" McCarter asked.

There was a short silence, then a hesitant answer. *"Oui."*

"Parlez-vous anglais?" McCarter asked. He could speak a little French, but the strong Marseilles accent was making it difficult for him.

"Yes, I speak English."

"Would you open the door?" Encizo requested. "We need to talk with you."

"Who are you?"

"Friends of Delgado," McCarter answered.

They heard the man on the other side of the door expel a breath of air. A moment later came the resounding clang of a bolt being slammed home.

"The bugger's gone and locked the door," the Briton exclaimed.

"Guess that means he doesn't want to speak to us."

"Yeah? We'll see about that."

McCarter took a couple of steps back, then launched his powerful frame at the door. His shoulder slammed into the edge, just above the halfway mark. The flimsy door was driven wide open and crashed back against the inner wall.

As McCarter barreled inside, his hand snatching the autopistol from beneath his coat, he caught a glimpse of a retreating figure. In the dimness of the poorly lit room, he made out the shape of a man running toward the open window in the back wall.

"No, you bloody well don't!"

McCarter's long legs enabled him to reach the man before Ferney could lay a hand on the window frame. The Phoenix pro closed a big hand over Ferney's collar and hauled him to a stop.

Encizo stepped into the room, closing the door behind him as best he could. He saw that the lock and bolt had been torn from the wood, so he dragged a heavy armchair in front of the door to hold it shut.

"See if there's more light," McCarter growled as he swung Ferney into a hard-backed chair.

Encizo found a switch beside the door. He flicked it and flooded the room with light.

One look at the untidy mess that passed as Ferney's living quarters made Encizo realize he would have been better leaving the room in darkness.

Ferney, who fitted Delgado's description, was thin and wiry, with the bony face of a man who apparently never had a decent meal. The Frenchman's features were almost gaunt. He stared first at McCarter, then at Encizo. He was scared, trying not to show it but making a lousy job of the effort.

"Why do a runner?" McCarter asked.

"Je ne comprends pas." Ferney shrugged.

"Cut the crap," Encizo said. "You understand fine. So come on, answer the question. Why were you running away?"

"I did not know who you were," Ferney replied.

"I said we were from Delgado," McCarter reminded him. "You do know Delgado? Of course you do, mate. You gave him some very important information a while back. That's why we're here."

"If you are from Delgado, you know all I had to tell. What more can I do than pass along information?"

"It isn't the passing of the information," Encizo explained. "It's the quality of it."

"And its authenticity," McCarter growled.

"Are you saying I gave Delgado false information? That is not true," Ferney bleated, his voice rising. He was starting to sweat, and his eyes darted nervously around the room. "What reason would I have for passing along false information?"

"How about money?" McCarter asked sharply, acting on impulse. He watched Ferney closely as he asked his question.

At the mention of money, Ferney became even more agitated. He scrubbed a pale hand across his unshaven jawline. "Money?" he repeated.

"They must be paying you well," McCarter said out of the blue. His remark was intended to catch Ferney off guard, and it did. The fleeting expression of guilt that flashed across Ferney's sweating face belied the innocence he professed.

"No one is paying me anything," he exclaimed, gesturing wildly with his thin hands. "Why should I take money for telling the truth?"

McCarter glanced in Encizo's direction, catching the Cuban's nod. Both Phoenix warriors were convinced now that Ferney had been passing information that had been concocted for Delgado's ears.

"Truth is a funny thing," Encizo observed. "It can have many meanings, and is genuine to one man but a lie to another."

"I do not understand," Ferney blustered, uncomfortable now and beginning to show desperation. He needed a way out. An escape.

That freedom was not forthcoming. Neither McCarter nor Encizo was about to make life easy for the man. Ferney had sold out to the other side, placing himself in the position of sacrificial pawn. Now he was finding that position less than appealing and becoming more dangerous with each passing second.

"Forget the bullshit," McCarter growled impatiently. He was beginning to get angry, and McCarter in an angry mood was something to behold. "Either give with the information, chum, or start counting how much time you have left."

Ferney shot an alarmed glance in the Briton's direction. He had been intimidated by the man, and McCarter's unpleasant manner was starting to rattle him. Ferney was wondering whether he had been wise to allow himself to become involved in Testarov's scheme. The problem was that Ferney, despite the large amount of money he had negotiated, feared the Russian as much as he did the Englishman. He was caught between two evils, with nowhere left to hide.

"Well?" Encizo asked, keeping his voice softer, almost gentle in comparison with McCarter's menacing tones. "The sooner we have what we came for, Ferney, the sooner we'll be out of your life."

"I might still rip his bleedin' throat out," McCarter threatened.

Ferney sprang from the chair, his eyes wide with fear.

"You must not make me speak. They would kill me if I..." His voice trailed away as he caught a flicker of movement at the open window.

"Please...no!" he shouted. "I told them nothing—"

McCarter glanced in the direction of the window, picking up on Ferney's agitation, and saw for himself the figure leaning in through the open frame with an automatic pistol in his hand. The muzzle was tracking in toward McCarter and Ferney.

The Briton exploded into action, lunging at the seemingly paralyzed Ferney, his arms reaching out to drag the man to the floor. As McCarter collided with Ferney, knocking the Frenchman to the floor, he heard the crack of a shot. The bullet whacked the edge of the table, sending splinters of wood into the air.

Close by, Encizo spotted the muzzle-flash of the intruder's gun. He flipped up the P-88's muzzle and returned fire, triggering a volley of shots that blasted the window frame to shreds and drove the would-be assassin back out of sight.

In the few seconds gained by Encizo's action, McCarter yanked Ferney to his feet and shoved him to the far side of the room.

"Nice friends you've got," the Briton said. "Does this happen often?"

Ferney started to reply, but his words were cut off as the door was forced open and the armchair was sent skittering across the room. A bulky figure stood framed in the doorway, an autorifle cradled in his arms. The weapon began firing, filling the room with its thunder and the deadly projectiles issuing from the muzzle. Bullets ripped into furniture and pounded the walls.

Acting out of pure instinct, the Phoenix warriors hit the floor again.

Ferney took longer to react, and his delay became fatal.

A number of bullets found their mark, crashing into the Frenchman's upper body. A short, stunned cry escaped Ferney's lips as the bullets drove him across the room. He fell, his limbs already losing their natural coordination. More bullets struck, tearing into Ferney's chest and neck. Blood began to spurt from a severed artery. Twitching like a stranded fish, Ferney struck the floor.

"Son of a bitch!" Encizo exclaimed.

He twisted his body around, triggering the P-88 in the direction of the killer framed in the doorway.

The subgunner caught a number of 9 mm slugs in his right shoulder. The impact threw him off balance, and his finger slipped briefly from the trigger of his weapon.

Encizo followed through, sending a second volley of shots into the gunman.

The second time, his aim was even truer, as the burst of deadly slugs hammered into the target's chest. The man staggered back into the passage, away from the door, then fell with a resounding crash.

McCarter had already moved, his eyes fixed on the back window. As Encizo triggered the P-88, McCarter caught movement at the window. Light glanced off the barrel of an autopistol as the gunman leaned forward.

"Gotcha!" McCarter whispered.

He leveled the P-88 and eased back on the trigger, sending the first of a trio of 9 mm slugs.

The gunman gave a startled grunt, his right arm whipping to one side as the slugs chewed into his flesh.

"Let's get out of here, Rafael," the Cockney yelled to his partner.

Encizo was bent over Ferney, checking for any sign of life. He found none. He broke away from the body and crossed the room to follow McCarter through the window and onto the fire escape beyond.

A figure lunged from the shadows, lashing out at McCarter. The Briton took a savage blow to the face. He pulled away before his assailant could strike again.

Encizo, coming through just behind his partner, saw the attack. He made out the figure of a taut-featured man, clad in a dark suit, bearing down on McCarter. The dull gleam of wet blood covered the man's right arm, evidence of McCarter's accurate shooting.

The Cuban moved in fast, bringing his P-88 up.

McCarter's attacker, despite his injury, struck again. As he moved toward McCarter, he reached inside his coat and pulled out a stubby dagger. He slashed viciously at the Briton.

Encizo's P-88 fired twice, sending a pair of 9 mm slugs into the attacker's chest, knocking him off balance and sending him crashing facedown on the fire escape.

"Thanks, chum," McCarter acknowledged.

"One thing for certain," Encizo said. "These guys didn't come from the tourist board to welcome us to Marseilles. I don't fancy hanging around to see if they have any buddies."

"Nor me," McCarter agreed.

The Phoenix commandos scrambled over the fire escape railing and made their way down the rusted, swaying iron ladder.

"This is getting to be a habit," McCarter muttered as they reached the ground. "Every time we ask a civil question, some bugger starts shooting. Do you think we're using the wrong deodorant or something?"

Encizo patted him on the arm. "Don't worry about it, buddy." He grinned. "It just comes with the territory is all. Now, let's get out of here."

They moved quickly along the shadowed alley that backed the building, making for the pool of light showing at the far end.

Before they had covered a third of the distance, armed men broke from the shadows, surrounding the

Phoenix warriors. A harsh voice rapped out a command in French, then repeated it in English.

"You will throw down your weapons immediately. If you refuse, we will open fire. Do it now, then place your hands against the wall and spread your legs."

"Who the hell is asking?" McCarter demanded.

"We are a special unit of the Marseilles Police Department. You are under arrest. Do not offer any resistance or we *will* open fire!"

McCarter and Encizo did as they were told. They were in no position to argue. Once they had thrown down their weapons, men moved in close to search them thoroughly and roughly.

After that both Stony Man commandos were handcuffed.

Surrounded by the grim-faced men of the police squad, McCarter and Encizo were marched out of the alley to a waiting police van. They were bundled inside, and the door was locked shut. After much frantic shouting in French, the van lurched forward, its gears clashing.

McCarter glanced across at Encizo.

"Well?" he demanded.

"I didn't say a damned thing," Encizo replied.

"Bloody well better not," the Briton muttered.

Encizo lapsed into a contemplative silence himself, well aware of the difficulty of their position. Such a turn of events was not going to go down too well back at the Farm. And Katz wasn't going to be overjoyed at the turn of events, either.

It was a hell of a first night in Marseilles, and Encizo wondered if it might be their last.

10

Karen Hoffe had joined the Phoenix warriors in Katz's hotel room to relate her side of the story, finishing up with the confrontation in Cornwall.

"Had you been suspicious before the London trip?" Katz asked. "Had this happened before?"

"Recently?"

"Let's say since you were involved with us in Germany."

Karen shook her head. "Nothing concrete," she said. "Just the occasional feeling I was being watched. But that is often the case in our kind of work. It was only after I had landed in England that I knew for certain."

Calvin James interjected, "Harper's theory is starting to make some kind of sense."

Harper was McCarter's cover name for the mission.

Katz nodded. "We have to consider it along with any other notions. One of our priorities is to establish, if we can, where the connection between Karen and Gary was realized. And by whom."

"Maybe your call to base will get us some help," Manning suggested.

He was referring to the telephone call Katz had put through to Kurtzman back at Stony Man. The Bear was, even at that very moment, running a check via his computers on everyone connected with the mission in Germany. His legendary skill at the keyboard enabled him to gain access to the most secure computer banks in the world. He could probe and sift and collate information from dozens of sources. In essence, if a piece of information existed, somewhere, anywhere, Kurtzman would get to it.

Karen stood up. "Do you mind if I return to my room for the present? I realize you have things to talk about which don't concern me. It will be better if I am out of your way."

"Yes, that would be a help," Katz affirmed. "Give us a little time to organize ourselves, Karen, then we can get together."

Manning saw Karen to her room. When he returned, Katz motioned him to sit down. The Canadian sensed the strained atmosphere in the room.

"Something wrong?" he asked.

"There isn't an easy way to say this, Gary," Katz began.

The Israeli's reluctant manner aroused Manning's suspicions. He glanced at James, who looked away after a few seconds.

And then it hit Manning.

"No way!" he objected forcibly. "I don't give a damn what you think. Karen wouldn't be part of any conspiracy against us. Katz, you've no right even thinking it."

"Gary, I have every right," the Phoenix commander argued. "When there is a threat to the security of Phoenix Force, I have to explore every avenue. Every possibility, no matter how distasteful it might appear.

"Remember one thing. My concern is the collective safety of the group, and as such I must look at things objectively."

"Is it objective to place Karen under suspicion?" Manning asked.

"Katz hasn't exactly done that, Gary," James pointed out. "All he's suggested is . . ."

"I can read between the lines, Cal," Manning snapped. "I just don't like what I'm hearing."

Before Katz could make any further reply, the telephone rang, James picked it up. "It's for you, Kaplan," he said after a moment, and held the phone out to Katz.

"Kaplan speaking."

Katz listened to the caller, his face turning grim as he listened. "Thanks for the call, Delgado. Get back to me if you pick up anything else." The Israeli put down the phone and turned to face the others.

"What is it?" Manning asked.

"Rafael and David have been arrested by a special squad of the Marseilles police," he said. "From what Delgado has got from his informants, they were involved in a firefight at Ferney's place. Ferney is dead, and so are two unidentified foreigners."

"Where are the guys now?" James asked.

"We don't know that yet. The special squad operates from a number of safehouses. Delgado is trying to locate them now."

"So what do we do?" Manning inquired.

"First we contact Stony Man. Hal needs to know what's happened. Maybe he can pull strings."

"Like the ones he pulled getting us permission to operate in France?" Manning asked dryly.

Katz glanced at him, a rebuke on his lips. Then he recalled the pressure Manning was under, due to Karen's involvement with the mission. He allowed the Canadian's sarcasm to slip by unchallenged.

Picking up the phone, Katz dialed the long number sequence that would connect him, via satellite link and scramblers, to Stony Man Farm. The line would be secure and would make Brognola sound as if he were in the same room.

When the Farm answered, Katz asked for Brognola, top priority. The Fed was on the line in under a minute.

"We were just going to call you," Brognola said. "Bear has come up with something that might answer your questions."

"Good," Katz said. "First let me give you something to think about."

"Go ahead."

"A special squad of the Marseilles police have Harper and Cicero in custody. They were involved in a firefight and were arrested shortly after. We don't even know where they are being held."

Brognola sighed. "I'll get our diplomatic people on it right away."

"Are they the same ones who're trying to get us official backing for our mission?"

"Yeah."

"Well, ask them to speed things up a little, or we may have to join the foreign legion."

"Do our best, Kaplan, you know that. Now, here's our readout from the computer. You might not like this."

"I'm listening."

"The Bear ran a make on all the contacts you made during your German mission. Out of them all, only one name comes out with a question mark next to it."

"Who is it?"

"Martin Kohler."

Katz was momentarily shaken. "Explain."

"Kohler has gone missing. He simply vanished from his BND unit about three months back. The Germans mounted an exhaustive search, but they couldn't find him. Martin Kohler has just vanished."

"Does anyone have any theories?"

Brognola grunted derisively. "Plenty of those, though everyone's just trying to help. He may have been snatched by a terrorist group or foreign agents. Or he's defected. Or been killed and his body dumped."

"I would have expected some kind of demand by now if he'd been kidnapped," Katz speculated.

"Kidnappers usually want something when they grab a hostage. They don't do it for fun."

"We were thinking along those lines ourselves," Brognola said.

"Of course, there could be a logical explanation for Kohler's disappearance," Katz went on, "but the longer the silence is maintained, the less likely that remains valid."

Brognola cleared his throat. "If Martin Kohler—for whatever reason—is with a hostile group, he could give them a lot of information about you guys."

"Don't remind me on that score," the Israeli said.

"The Bear is still digging," the Fed informed the Phoenix Force commander. "As soon as we have anything, we'll get it to you. In the meantime, I'll see if I can kick some ass and get you guys that clearance with the French authorities."

"Thanks," Katz said, and broke the connection.

It took him no time at all to repeat the conversation to Manning and James. The Canadian failed to conceal his relief. "I told you Karen had nothing to do with this mess."

"Gary, all we know at the moment is that Kohler has disappeared. It doesn't necessarily mean that he's implicated."

"It does to me," Manning insisted. "You were quick enough to condemn Karen. So if that's the way we play the game, then Martin Kohler is just as suspect. Think about it, Katz. The guy vanishes, and then we start getting fingered. Makes sense to me."

"Never mind about Kohler," James interrupted. "What about David and Rafael? They're the ones who need our help right now."

Katz nodded. "Cal's right. I suggest we get over to Delgado's place. See if he's come up with any information on where David and Rafael might be. We'll pick up a taxi in case the rental car has been put under surveillance."

"Give me a minute," Manning said, and left the room.

As they got ready, James said, "Gary's really cut up about Karen."

"I know that, Cal. My feelings can't be allowed to cloud my judgment, though. I have to consider everyone's safety, even if it means upsetting a few people."

"Yeah, I know, Katz." James gave him a quick smile. "You know what they say—it's hell at the top."

Ten minutes later the three Phoenix warriors left the hotel and picked up a taxi. Katz gave the driver Delgado's address, and the vehicle moved away.

As soon as the taxi left, two men climbed out of a car parked in the hotel lot. They looked around idly for a minute, as though they were in no great hurry, then made their way inside the hotel.

11

The Marseilles Opera House gave the city its music, but the area around the building was distinctly on a lower level. The dim streets were given over to bars and ladies of questionable virtue.

Phoenix Force alighted from their taxi. Manning paid off the driver, who tried to con him for double the fare until the Canadian gave him a mouthful of choice French obscenities. Realizing he wasn't dealing with a tourist straight off the boat, the scowling driver snatched the money and drove away.

"This is where Delgado lives?" James asked.

Katz nodded. "He has an apartment over that bar."

"The guy certainly likes to mix with the natives," the Chicago hardass muttered.

"Best way to blend in," Manning commented.

The Phoenix trio made their way along the street, easing through the noisy throng. Music blared out from the bars. People called out to each other in greeting and conversed loudly. There was laughter and a general air of brashness. Marseilles is noted for its outward-looking inhabitants. They have a lust for life that spills over into their work and play, making the city a vibrant, often raucous place.

Katz paused outside the bar he had indicated. He entered a door off to the side, followed by the others. They found themselves in a dim passage, which eventually opened onto a paved courtyard. Stone steps led up to a gallery. It was a little less noisy there, with the street sounds subdued.

It was the comparative calm that enabled the Force to pick up the raised voices. They were coming from the gallery. A man suddenly yelled. There was the sound of a blow. Glass smashed.

"Something tells me Delgado is involved in that," Manning said.

"Let's check it out," James suggested. "We were going up there anyway."

The Phoenix warriors sprinted up the steps. Light spilled out from an open door, throwing a pale glow across the gallery. The sounds of conflict grew louder.

Manning reached the door first. He peered inside. It was the main room of the apartment. And it was Delgado's, all right.

Their contact was in the middle of the conflict, his arms held by a pair of hefty men while two others rained blows to his face and body.

Katz and James stepped inside the room just behind Manning. James slammed the door shut with a loud bang, drawing the attention of the quartet attacking Delgado.

"Who are you?" one of the four snarled. He was a large man with huge fists and a swarthy, sunburned complexion. His companions were similar in build and looks.

"Friends of Delgado," Katz answered in perfect French. "Friends who do not appreciate him being attacked by a bunch of louts in his own home."

"You do not look like a Frenchman," the big man said.

"Friend, you don't look like the asshole you obviously are," James remarked, also speaking French.

The pair restraining Delgado let him go, shoving him to the floor. Delgado, his face streaming blood that had soaked the front of his shirt, moved to slump against the wall.

"If you bastards are friends of this shit, maybe you are the ones responsible for Ferney's death," one of the men said.

"I don't expect you to believe me," Katz replied, "but we had nothing to do with his death."

"Liar!"

"Why don't you guys just get out," Manning suggested.

"We will. After settling with you."

The big man advanced across the room, his large hands closed into massive fists. He started swinging before he reached Katz, but the Israeli had no problem avoiding the heavy punches. The moment the Frenchman was within Katz's reach, he swung his prosthesis in a glittering arc that terminated against the guy's jaw. The hard tips of the steel hooks ripped bloody gouges deep into flesh. Blood bubbled to the surface in a red flood. As the startled thug clapped a hand to his bleeding face, Katz drove the toe of his shoe between the man's legs, crushing his testicles. Howling in agony, the big man folded, and Katz helped him continue his downward movement. He sledged his left fist into the skull, just behind the ear. The blow put the man on his knees, and Katz hit him again, pitching him facedown on the floor.

Even as Katz was dealing with the big man, the other three thugs had joined the fray.

A pockmarked man, whose face gleamed with sweat, lunged at Manning, a slim-bladed knife suddenly appearing in his right hand. He advanced on the Canadian, his eyes glittering, a thin smile on his wet lips. The razor-sharp blade cut the air in tight little movements. Manning held his ground. His attention was on the guy's face, knowing that the eyes would indicate the moment he was about to strike. The Phoenix warrior read his man correctly. He caught the hard gleam of anticipation that glazed the thug's eyes and switched his own gaze to the knife as it commenced its strike. Manning's left hand shot out, his powerful grip closing over the opponent's right wrist. The Canadian was no slouch when it came to muscle power. The French thug found he was powerless to stop his arm being deflected from its path. The moment he had the knife under control, Manning drove his right fist at the thug's throat, his knuckles crunching against the windpipe. The force of the blow stopped the thug in his tracks, and he began to choke violently. Without pause Manning continued his move, twisting the guy's wrist until the pain made him drop the knife. Manning shoved the man hard, slamming him into the wall beside the door.

Calvin James found himself confronted by the remaining pair of thugs. They came for him in a rush, neither man in tune with the other. The black warrior took out the first one with a powerful snap-kick, planting the sole of his shoe in the unsuspecting thug's face. There was a sodden crunching sound, and blood flowered across the man's face. Recovering from his first strike, James whipped a hard backfist against the side of the second man's face. The man's head jerked to the side. Before he could even think about what had hit him, James stepped in close and hammered the point of his elbow into the exposed ribs on the left side of the body. The thug gave a startled cry as bone cracked. James took him out of his misery with a clubbing blow across the back of the neck, stretching the guy out on the floor.

The moment he had dealt with his opponent, Katz went to Delgado's side. The contact man was barely conscious, his face a mass of angry bruises and deep gashes. One eye had already begun to swell shut. His lips were badly split. Blood was streaming from his broken nose and lacerated gums. As Katz cradled the beaten man in his arms, Delgado glanced up at him. "I told you it was a tough town," he mumbled.

"Just take it easy," Katz soothed. "We'll get you to a doctor."

Delgado moaned in pain, pressing his hands to his sides.

"Who are these guys?" James asked, kneeling beside Delgado.

"Local gangsters. The Marseilles Mafia. These fellows play dirty, guys, so watch your backs."

"Oh, great," James said. "Now we have the neighborhood Mob on our trail, as well."

"Let's get Delgado out of here," Katz said. To the contact man, he said, "Do you have a car?"

"Dark blue Renault out back. Keys in pocket."

Manning had searched the thugs and relieved them of various weapons. The injured gangsters were in no shape to retaliate. They remained where they had fallen, in various states of unconsciousness.

Katz and James helped Delgado to his feet and assisted him from the apartment. Delgado directed them along the gallery to steps that led down to the rear of the building, where a rough patch of ground served as a place to park cars and dump trash. The contact man's car was parked close to a wall. Using the keys taken from Delgado's pocket, Katz opened the car door. Manning reached inside to unlock the other doors. Katz eased onto the rear seat with Delgado, while Manning and James climbed in the front. The Canadian started the Renault.

"Where are we going?" he asked.

"Turn left at the street," Delgado spoke up. "Drive to the top of the hill, then take a right at the junction. I will guide you."

"What's our destination?" Katz asked.

"A friend. A doctor I can trust."

"Now, there's something that is spread pretty damned thin at the moment," Gary Manning said with a trace of bitterness in his voice. *"Trust."*

12

When the van transporting McCarter and Encizo arrived at its destination, the Phoenix warriors were hauled out and moved, on the run, through the darkness and into a building. After they were hustled along a stone passage, then down a flight of stone steps, they were shoved into a chilly cellar illuminated by strip lights. Their captors slammed them into hard chairs, handcuffing their wrists to steel tubes set in the stone floor. Then the heavy door banged shut on them, and they were left alone.

They remained in isolation for the next three hours. Both Phoenix warriors were aware of the setup. This was the softening-up period. The prisoner, in strange surroundings, away from the familiar, was placed in an empty room with nothing but his thoughts for company. No one would come near him for a period. During that time the captive's weaknesses would generate unease and throw him off balance. He would begin to imagine all kinds of terrible things happening to him when his captors eventually showed their faces. His own frailties would work against him, laying him open to all kinds of manipulation.

Rafael Encizo had firsthand knowledge of this kind of treatment. His time spent in the infamous El Principe, Castro's political prison, had taught Encizo a great deal about psychological torture. He had survived what the Communist guards had thrown at him, and in the end he had escaped to freedom. But he still carried the memories of that time around with him. They would never go—and at times like these, they flooded back, giving him the strength to fight whatever his new captors might push him into.

The situation did little to affect David McCarter. The Briton's capacity for enduring physical and mental deprivation was well-known. He walked into and through any and every conflict with the confident knowledge that he would survive it by some means or other. McCarter assessed each new situation as it occurred, adjusting his body and mind to that particular episode. Chameleonlike, he changed to suit the day and allowed little to upset him. He was a true survivor. Bending when the need arose. Staying firm at the crucial moment, and never letting any odds deter him.

The Phoenix commandos accepted their situation now, aware that they were in for a long wait. They used the time to recharge their batteries, relaxing as much as physically possible under the circumstances. With the insight of past experience, they remained silent, not wanting to give any information away by careless talk. Hidden microphones could easily pick up anything they said.

Time ran slowly. The chill in the cellar seeped into the Phoenix warriors' bones slowly. McCarter figured it had to be coming up to midnight. When they had been searched, the police had confiscated both their watches. By now, he guessed, Katz and the others would be wondering what had happened, and they might even be out looking for them.

He glanced across at Encizo, and the Cuban gave a half grin of encouragement.

There was sound beyond the door of their cell. It swung open and men appeared. They crossed to where McCarter and Encizo were seated. The handcuffs were removed and the Phoenix pair escorted from the room. They were taken upstairs and along a passage, then through a door that led to another passage. This one was carpeted. A door was opened, and McCarter and Encizo stepped into a furnished room.

A tall man was bending over a table on which lay papers and photographs. A map was pinned to a board fixed on one wall. The door behind the Phoenix pair closed. The man at the table straightened and turned to face McCarter and Encizo.

"I'm Rene Giraud," he said in flawless English. He glanced at McCarter. "You will be Mr. Harper. Your companion, Mr. Cicero. Please take a seat, gentlemen. And welcome to France."

The man in charge of the police squad was tall, rangy, with blue eyes and a deep tan. His light brown hair was thick and sun bleached. He looked more like a lifeguard off the beach at Malibu than a cop from Marseilles. But for all that, he was no slouch. Giraud ran his squad with an iron fist, and there was no doubting the man's innate hardness.

McCarter slumped into a deep armchair. He was still working out what was going on. Until it was fully explained, he saw no reason why he shouldn't be comfortable.

Working from the same basis, Encizo sat down himself.

Giraud leaned against the table at his back and allowed himself a slight smile.

"I know who you are now," he explained. "The authorities have been in touch with my superiors, who in turn passed along the information to me. It appears that your government has been granted permission for you and your colleagues to proceed with investigations. I have been told to offer any assistance you may require."

"How long ago did this information get into your hands?" Encizo asked.

"Only within the last half an hour," Giraud said. A wry grin etched itself across his face. "You were released the moment I had confirmation."

McCarter stared at the French cop. Giraud held his gaze unflinchingly. For a while the two men sized each other up. "Okay," McCarter said. "I believe he's telling us the truth."

"Fine," Encizo snapped. "Can we get some action around here?"

"What kind of action?" Giraud asked.

"A telephone for a start," the Cuban said. "I need to call my colleagues."

"They are already on their way," Giraud answered. "Since you left your hotel earlier this evening, there have been a number of developments."

"Such as?" McCarter demanded.

"Your three friends confronted members of the local underworld who were attacking your contact man at his apartment. They dealt with that and took Delgado to a doctor friend. When they returned to the hotel some hours later, they found that the young woman who arrived with you had disappeared from her room. There were signs of a struggle. Shortly after, some of my people reached them at the hotel. They should be with us soon."

"Great," McCarter grumbled. "This mission goes from bad to shitty in effortless bounds."

"I could say the same thing about my own situation," Giraud said, with a little snappiness in his tone.

"Oh?" Encizo commented.

The Frenchman had picked up a thick folder from the table. He waved it in the direction of the Phoenix pair.

"What's that?" McCarter asked.

Giraud banged the file down on the table to emphasize his words. "We have been compiling a dossier on Ferney for over a month. Taking photographs of his meetings. Of anyone he had contact with. We were almost ready to move in. Then you show up, and now Ferney is dead.''

"Don't blame us for that," McCarter replied abruptly. "We almost ended up in the same condition as Ferney. Remember those buggers were shooting at us, also."

"All we wanted to do was talk to the man," Encizo said. "We needed a little information."

Giraud grunted in annoyance. He pulled a pack of Gauluois from his pocket and took one out. After he had lit it, he leaned his shoulder against the wall, drawing heavily on the cigarette. His hard blue eyes flicked back and forth between McCarter and Encizo.

"Maybe I should throw you pair back in the cellar and keep you there for a while," he said.

"What would that achieve?" Encizo questioned.

Giraud smiled through a cloud of cigarette smoke. "It would give me a great deal of satisfaction."

"That's always been the trouble with the French," McCarter said. "No sense of humour."

"And I suppose you British have plenty?" Giraud retorted.

McCarter nodded. "Of course. With our climate we have to."

Giraud laughed. He pulled up a chair and sat facing the Phoenix pair across the table. "We can tough this out forever," he said. "Or we can work together. Now, I'm no diplomat. I don't promise to always keep my temper, but I'm prepared to try." He held out his hands, palms turned up. "Well?"

"I'm thinking about it," McCarter said, "but why not? What about it, Cicero?"

Encizo inclined his head. "I'm game."

"Good," Giraud concluded. "Let's find you some food and drink. Do you like bouillabaisse?"

"Never had it," Encizo said.

"I have," McCarter acknowledged. "Has to be made correctly or it's bloody terrible."

"I can promise you ours is superb. One of my men has a recipe handed down through three generations, all local. Come, we will go upstairs."

As Giraud led them from the room, heading for the kitchen, Encizo nudged his partner's arm.

"What is it?" he whispered.

"Bouillabaisse? It's fish soup or stew, depending on how you view it. They put *rascasse*, scorpion fish, in it, besides eel, scampi, crabs and lobsters. You'll like it."

Encizo took McCarter's word. Inwardly he wasn't so sure. He decided to reserve judgement until he'd sampled the dish.

KATZ, JAMES AND MANNING arrived at the house ten minutes later. They were brought to the kitchen, where McCarter and Encizo were being introduced to the delights of bouillabaisse. The Phoenix warriors each had a steaming bowl of the fish delicacy. There were also bottles of chilled white wine and freshly baked crusty bread. After the introductions had been made, the new arrivals joined the others at the large kitchen table, where more bowls of bouillabaisse were placed before them.

After tasting the dish, Katz nodded his approval.

Gary Manning toyed with his meal. His attention was elsewhere, which was natural in the circumstances.

"Lomas," Giraud said to Manning. "We will do all we can to find out who took the woman and where they have her. Marseilles may be a large city, but we have our sources of information."

"I think it's time we traded the information we have between us," Katz suggested. "Better we all know what the other party is doing."

"Agreed," Giraud said.

"As you are probably aware from what your superiors told you, we handle certain matters for the U.S. government. Over a number of years we've made some enemies. We have reason to believe certain of those enemies have drawn us to Marseilles as part of a plan to exact revenge."

"Who are these people?" Giraud asked.

"KGB," Katz stated.

"The Russians? Here in Marseilles?"

"Somewhere. Keeping well hidden—except for the ones who attacked Harper and Cicero. You see, we know for a fact that Ferney was used to pass information to our contact man, and that information—nicely concocted to attract us—came from the Soviets. We also learned that there are some Libyans in the area, somehow connected to the Russians."

Giraud's eyes sparkled. "During our surveillance of Ferney, he made contact with a group of North Africans. They are, in turn, connected with a ship berthed at one of the docks. Perhaps these are the people you were informed about. Give me a few moments."

Giraud left the room. He returned shortly with a manila envelope in his hands. He opened it and took out a bundle of photographs. He passed them along the table. They were black-and-white ten-by-eight-inch prints. Without exception they were excellent shots, the images sharp and detailed.

Picking them up, Katz went through the photographs one by one. He had only scanned the first three when he paused to inspect one closely.

"You got something?" James asked.

Katz simply passed him the photo. The black warrior took it and turned it around, his eyes searching the faces in the group of six men caught by the camera.

"It's him," he said softly. "Isn't it?"

Katz nodded. "Yes, it's him."

The others gathered round. Katz placed the photograph on the table and turned it so that the whole of Phoenix Force could see.

"It's Martin Kohler," McCarter confirmed.

"You had better hear the rest," Katz said. "While you and Cicero were out, we received a call from home. They were responding to a request we had made concerning the possibility of someone having marked us for the KGB. Someone who knew us and had personal experience of working with us. They came up with the fact that Martin Kohler vanished from his BND unit over a month ago. No one had been able to locate him.''

"Until he turns up in Marseilles," Manning said.

"That one there is Ferney," McCarter pointed out.

Giraud indicated three other figures. "The North Africans," he explained.

"What is interesting," Katz said, "is the man on Ferney's left."

"Means nothing to me," Manning said.

"I can't put a name to him," James added, "but the guy is familiar. Where have I seen him, Kaplan?"

"The Philippines," Katz explained. "That is Leoni Testarov. The KGB man who ran the Morkrie Dela team during the attempt to assassinate Aquino."

"Now it's all coming together," Manning said. "The scenario fits. It *was* a come-on all the time. A KGB scam to draw us out so they could kill us."

"Didn't I say so?" McCarter commented. "The odd ones out are the Libyans. How do they figure in this?"

"As I mentioned, it may have something to do with the freighter berthed at one of the quays," Giraud reminded them. "We've seen the North Africans go aboard a number of times."

"Wonder what they're up to?" James asked.

"Why don't we go take a look?" McCarter suggested. As usual his idea was to go straight in and ask questions later.

"Yes, why not," Giraud agreed. He looked at his watch. "We could go in just before dawn. Catch them off guard."

McCarter looked well pleased. "I really do like this bloke."

"Do you think Testarov is the one who took Karen?" Manning asked Katz.

"It's possible," the Israeli said.

"Don't you have any idea where these people are hiding out?" Manning asked Giraud.

"The North Africans were staying at a hotel up until a week ago. Then one morning they checked out and vanished. The photograph of them with Ferney and this man you call the Russian was taken two days before they disappeared."

"No contact with Ferney since then?" Encizo probed.

Giraud shook his head. "None. We'd kept a close watch on him. The only person of significance he spoke to was Delgado."

"Let's go for the Libyans," Katz said. He turned to Giraud. "Will you arrange it?"

The French cop nodded. "Of course."

"All we have are handguns," Katz said. "Can you provide us with extra firepower?"

"Certainly. Just come with me." He led the way from the kitchen to a back room. Inside was an impressive array of weaponry.

"Please help yourselves," Giraud said. "I'll leave you to it while I set up our visit."

The French-made Mab Model PA-15 automatic pistol was the universal choice for a handgun, while there were at least three SMGs to choose from. The Uzi was there, alongside the MP-5, and the 9 mm MAT-49. The MAT, French designed and built, was of the blowback type, capable of a cyclic rate of 600 RPM. An unusual feature of the MAT was the forward-folding magazine housing, which enabled the full magazine to be swung in line with the barrel. That feature reduced the bulk of the weapon while it was being carried. The magazine housing also served as a foregrip, a handy design that gave the user better control while firing, as the MAT-49 could only be fired on full-auto. Despite the limited firing mode, the MAT had been a firm favorite with the French military and police ever since its introduction in 1949.

Katz helped himself to an Uzi. After a little deliberation, Calvin James chose the Israeli weapon. Gary Manning went for an MP-5, which was Encizo's natural choice, the H&K being his standard SMG. No one was too surprised when McCarter picked one of the MAT-49s. The weapon suited the brash Cockney. It had similar characteristics. Like the Briton, the SMG was rugged and uncompromising. It did its job without the need for frills and fancy gadgetry.

Once they had picked their weapons, the Force checked and loaded them, adding extra magazines, which they dropped into their pockets.

When Giraud returned, Phoenix Force was armed and ready.

"We have a couple of cars," the undercover officer told them. "If you wish, one can be at your disposal. I am taking three men along with me."

"Lead the way," McCarter said.

"I see you have chosen a French weapon," Giraud commented.

"I like your wine, as well," the Briton retorted, "but it doesn't mean I'm about to apply for citizenship."

Giraud was not thrown by the Briton's snappy reply. "Not to worry," he replied. "We are not that desperate for more immigrants."

"I like that." James grinned.

"If you are all ready, we will go," Giraud said.

13

The Marseilles docks had been eventually rebuilt after their destruction by the Germans during the Second World War. In the intervening years the security of employment on the docks declined, due to a number of factors. The world shipping slump added to the misfortune of Marseilles, and though it still maintains its position as the main French port of the Mediterranean, some of the docks lie deserted and idle.

According to Giraud, the dock where the Libyans' vessel was berthed was one of those that had been shut down for a number of years. When they reached the main dock area, the French officer showed his ID to the security guard, and the two cars were allowed through the access gate. Giraud's car led the way along the quayside in the early-morning's chill light. A hazy mist drifted in off the ocean, pale tendrils floating just above the water.

Giraud's car drew to a stop beside a stack of rusting steel girders. He climbed out and waved Katz's car down. Manning, who was driving, braked and cut the motor.

"We walk from here," the French officer said.

The Force piled out of the car and fell in with Giraud and his men.

Ahead of them the docks lay silent and deserted. This was the section that had been closed due to lack of business. Water lapped against the pilings of bleak, empty quays. Debris littered the dock, and pieces of abandoned equipment lay scattered about.

The group rounded the end of a high stack of rusted fuel drums. Giraud, in the lead, came to an abrupt halt. He swore forcibly in his native tongue.

Katz moved to his side swiftly. "What's wrong?" he asked.

"It was there," the French cop said. "At the end quay."

The freighter had gone. The quay was empty.

Giraud stared at the deserted dock. "Damn!" he muttered. "They must have slipped away during the night."

"Didn't you have anyone watching her?" Manning asked.

"Of course." Giraud bristled, glaring at the Canadian. "If he failed to report, there can be only one explanation."

There was movement in the shadows behind them, and one of Giraud's team appeared. They spoke in low undertones.

"For those not familiar with the language," Giraud said, "although the ship has gone, there are still people in the warehouse. A number of North Africans and some French nationals. They are armed. It appears they are clearing out the warehouse.''

''Wonder what they've got to hide?'' Encizo asked.

''We will go and find out,'' Giraud said. ''Kaplan, you and your men stay together. I will take in my team.''

Katz nodded. The strategy made sense. Phoenix Force were more than familiar with each other's way of operating, as would be the French team.

''Which part of the warehouse do you want us to cover?''

''There is another set of access doors at the far end,'' Giraud explained. ''Also, along the north side of the building is a small door. If you will handle those doors, my men and I will tackle the main entrance here on the dock.''

''Fine,'' Katz affirmed. ''How long before we move in?''

''We will allow fifteen minutes for everyone to get in position. Let us synchronize watches.''

After that had been done, Giraud checked that everyone was ready.

''We hit in fifteen minutes from now. Go!''

Katz led the Force along the deserted dock to where they were able to cut along the side of the warehouse block. They moved fast but in silence, with Katz leading and McCarter at the rear. When they reached the end of the building, Katz held up a hand while he checked the way ahead.

There was a wide concrete apron where vehicles were able to park once they had entered the dock facility. At that time of the morning, the place was deserted. A couple of semitrailers were parked up near the security fence.

Katz scanned the area. He saw nothing to arouse his suspicions, but that didn't mean they were safe. He waited a couple of minutes longer.

"Seems clear enough," he said over his shoulder. "We'll take it a step at a time. There are loading ramps jutting out from each warehouse unit. We'll move down the line using them. One man goes first, then signals the others if and when the coast is clear."

Katz made the first ramp without incident. After a few seconds he waved the all clear. James and Encizo joined him, then Manning. McCarter waited until Katz had moved to the next ramp before he scooted across.

By that method the Force advanced along the warehouse block until they were all gathered behind the second-closest ramp.

"David, you and Cal take the rear access," Katz ordered. "The rest of us will head along to the side door."

McCarter tilted his head in acknowledgment, and Katz made the run to the last ramp and crouched in its shadow. He was about to wave the others to join him when he caught sight of a huddled shape against the base of the ramp wall. He brought the Uzi round in a swift movement, finger touching the trigger, and then realized he wouldn't be needing a gun.

He was looking at a corpse. Something told him it would be Giraud's missing man. The Israeli turned and waved the others to join him. The moment they were with him, Katz indicated the body.

James knelt over it. He looked, and after a moment, his face set. There was an expression of disgust in his eyes.

"The bastards," he whispered.

Katz, who had knelt beside the black warrior, took a look at the corpse and reacted in a similar fashion. The Phoenix warriors were used to death in its many forms. They had seen sights none of them would readily forget, but they had just seen another.

"What's wrong?" McCarter asked, sensing the unease among his partners. He glanced at the dead man. "Jesus, what bloody sicko did that?"

Giraud's man had been finally killed by a savage knife cut that had opened his throat. Before that, however, someone had spent some considerable time using that knife to inflict a series of hideous mutilations to the wretched man's face and body that were not only totally unnecessary, but also beyond anything a stable mind could conjure up.

"If the guy who did this ended up in court, some liberal lawyer would argue he ought to be let off," James said, failing to keep the anger from his voice. "It's crazy even thinking about letting a creep who could do this out on the streets again."

"Something tells me this one won't reach court," Manning said with feeling. What he was thinking was that Karen might be in this guy's hands next.

"Let's ease up," Katz said. "We've got a time limit to beat."

McCarter patted James on the shoulder. "Come on, chum, time to go." The Cockney rebel led the way along the base of the ramp. At the far end the pair checked out the loading dock and the warehouse doors, then climbed up onto the dock and vanished from sight.

Katz turned to Manning and Encizo. "We've seven minutes left to get in position. Time to move."

As they crept away from the loading ramp, Gary Manning found himself turning to glance at the mutilated corpse for one last time. He found it difficult to erase Karen's face from his mind, partly because he was blaming himself for bringing her to Marseilles and giving their opposition the chance to abduct her.

14

McCarter and James reached the warehouse with less than a minute to go before countdown. They had worked their way across the loading bay to the high corrugated steel doors only to find them closed and locked. McCarter prowled back and forth while James examined a smaller access door set in the wall beside the main doors. The black Phoenix warrior nodded to himself as he peered at the lock. He glanced at his watch and saw that the deadline was almost on them.

"You set?" he asked the Briton.

"Why? You found a key?"

"Funny guy," James said. He swung back toward the wooden access door and put all his considerable energy into a powerful snap-kick that planted the sole of his shoe against the frame of the door just above the lock.

Calvin James worked out regularly, perfecting his martial-arts techniques. He spent hours pounding away at wooden practice dummies with hands and feet, increasing his speed and inner strength. He had learned the age-old methods of concentrating all of one's energy in a single blow, channeling every ounce of force to the point of contact. The evidence of his long hours' working out showed in the way the door sprang open as the frame splintered around the lock.

"Remind me not to do anything to upset you," McCarter joked as he and James went in through the now-open door.

As they entered, they parted company, breaking left and right, crouching as they took in the layout of the vast warehouse.

The section they were in was filled with high rows of containers, cartons, barrels storing all kinds of merchandise from electronic equipment to cases of Scotch whiskey.

The Phoenix pair were able to conceal themselves behind the stacked goods as they heard the sound of men running in their direction. They heard agitated voices, as well, in a language that was unmistakably Arabic.

"Sounds like our desert chums are at home," McCarter said.

"Don't expect a welcome," James replied.

The sound of the approaching Libyans grew closer. James moved across to where McCarter waited behind a high stack of boxes. The commandos stood back-to-back, listening, waiting, weapons cocked and ready.

Even though he was watching out for the Libyans, their sudden appearance in the aisle between the stacks of boxes, no more than fifteen feet away, caught James by surprise.

There were three of them, swarthy-looking men dressed in casual clothing, all carrying AK-74s with the distinctive orange-colored magazine.

James nudged the Briton in the ribs to draw his attention, and when McCarter turned, James pointed out the armed trio.

A hungry grin curved the Cockney's mouth.

"Let's take the mothers," James whispered.

"Why, Calvin," McCarter admonished, "that sounded positively belligerent."

"Yeah? Well it damned well was, 'cause I just keep recalling what these creeps did to Giraud's man."

Any decision about what James was going to do to the Libyans was postponed by a sudden burst of autofire from the far end of the warehouse. There was an instant burst of return fire.

The Libyans exchanged glances. They began to argue about what they should do. One, becoming increasingly annoyed with his partners, turned on his heel and advanced in the direction of the rear of the warehouse, still intent on discovering what had caused the disturbance.

He found out sooner than he had expected, spotting James and McCarter before the Phoenix pair could move to a fresh location.

The Libyan uttered a wild yell of anger, calling to his companions and triggering his AK-74 at the same time.

A long burst of 5.45 mm slugs hammered at the Phoenix pair, chewing into the wooden packing cases and filling the air with splinters.

McCarter and James parted company, ducking behind alternate rows of boxes.

The Cockney, his blood racing wildly at the impending action, peered around the end of the row and saw the Libyans fanning out along the aisle.

The Briton poked the MAT-49 around the edge of the crate and opened fire. His blast of full-auto fire slapped the closest Libyan off his feet in midstride. The howling man crashed to the floor in a bloody heap, his AK-74 flying from his numb fingers and clattering across the concrete.

The Libyan who had opened fire on the Phoenix pair caught sight of his fatally hit Arab brother going down in a spray of blood. His rage at the butchery of a Libyan freedom fighter overwhelmed any thoughts of personal safety. He moved in the direction he had seen the black man go, his assault rifle held ready. Whatever else happened, even if he died, he would take one of the unbelievers with him. They were the cause of world unrest and the isolation of the Islamic nations. The holy war against the evil of the U.S.A. was the most righteous that a follower of Islam could undertake. To die for the cause was the only true way to reach Allah.

With his mind fixed firmly on his glorious afterlife, the Libyan moved around the row of boxes, eyes searching for his target.

As the Libyan showed himself, Calvin James stepped into view, his Uzi tracking the lean figure.

The black muzzle of the AK-74 came on line a second later.

The air was split by the harsh crackle of autofire.

The Libyan felt something hard strike his chest and lower torso. He was pushed back by an invisible force, crashing against the row of boxes with enough force to rock them. Then he felt the deep burn of pain as 9 mm slugs cored into his flesh, tearing through organs and breaking bones. In the grip of sudden paralysis, he tumbled sideways, striking the floor with stunning impact. His breathing became labored, and blood surged from his slack mouth in the long moments before darkness smothered him.

The moment he had dealt with his opponent, McCarter hurried in the direction he'd seen James take. He rounded the line of boxes in time to see the black warrior dispatch the second of the trio.

The Brit's eye was caught by movement above and to one side of James. The third Libyan had scrambled over the top of the line of crates and was behind the black commando. The guy's AK-74 was already arcing around to line up on the exposed back.

McCarter had appeared in the second before the Libyan fired. There was no time to even shout a warning. McCarter did the next best thing. He brought the MAT-49's muzzle up and eased back on the trigger, keeping it there. The SMG spat out the remaining contents of its magazine in a continuous burst. The stream of 9 mm slugs caught the Libyan in the upper thighs and torso, shredding clothing and flesh alike. The screaming man was knocked off the crates in a bloody haze, his shattered body thrown across the warehouse floor. He landed hard, smashing his skull on the concrete as he hit. His bleeding body soon ceased all movement.

McCarter flipped out the empty magazine and put in a fresh one. He cocked the French SMG.

"Come on, Cal, let's see what else is going on."

KATZ, along with Manning and Encizo, encountered no opposition during the approach. They reached the single door in the side of the warehouse with thirty seconds to spare before the deadline. Encizo tried the handle carefully. It yielded, the door easing outward as the catch disengaged.

"Everyone ready?" Katz asked.

The others nodded.

The second hand on the Israeli's watch touched zero, and Katz touched Encizo's arm. The Cuban yanked open the door, and the Phoenix trio slipped inside.

They had entered about midway along the warehouse. To their left the vast building was filled by rows and stacks of goods.

The front section of the warehouse was less densely packed with merchandise. Directly across from them was a wood-and-glass-partitioned office block, located in the middle of the floor. On their right the open warehouse floor was practically empty, save for a couple of cars, a panel truck and over a dozen men involved in clearing away the debris left in an area that had obviously been used for some kind of work.

The men were a mixture of French and darker-skinned Arabic types. Some were carrying weapons, while others had leaned their guns against boxes or the outer walls of the offices.

Katz glanced in the direction of the half-open front doors. He was in time to see the distant figures of Giraud and his men entering.

Giraud shouted a command in French. Whatever he said had an instant effect on the men milling about the warehouse floor. Without thought or hesitation, they all went for their weapons. Those who were carrying them opened fire, while the others ran to where they had left their guns.

One of them, a lean, wild-eyed Libyan, caught sight of Katz and the others as he snatched up his AK-74. He began to yell in a loud, high voice, his words tumbling over themselves in his excitement as he warned the others.

Then his Russian autorifle was up and firing, spitting flame and 5.45 mm bullets at the Phoenix warriors.

"So much for tact and caution," Manning said, returning fire. His MP-5 spat 9 mm slugs at the yelling Libyan.

The fanatic Arab caught a chestful of Manning's fire. He went down, still screaming his defiance, until blood rose in his throat and choked off his outburst.

Encizo leveled his MP-5 at an advancing pair of autogunners as they turned their weapons in his direction. Hot slugs whacked the concrete floor around the Cuban as the moving thugs fired on the run. Encizo stood his ground, triggering the SMG only when he was satisfied that he had his targets on line. The Heckler and Koch stuttered loudly, sending a stream of deadly projectiles into the gunners. They were diverted from their forward momentum by the force of the bullets, their bodies shuddering under the impact. One stumbled blindly against his partner, and the pair crashed to the floor, bleeding bodies sprawling across the concrete.

A lone Libyan traded shots with Katz, then turned and ran for the cover of the office block. He kicked open a door and ducked inside, seconds before a blast from Katz's Uzi shattered windows and splintered wood panels. Bullets flew across the office, thudding into the far wall. The Libyan suddenly appeared again, poking the muzzle of his AK-74 through one of the shattered windows. He began to fire at the dodging figure of the Israeli, his shots whining off the concrete. Then his weapon clicked empty. The Libyan cursed under his breath, fumbling to release the empty magazine, aware that Katz was getting closer. Still he persisted, dropping the empty magazine as it came free. He started to shove in a fresh magazine. At that moment Katz reached the office block and flattened himself against the wall for a moment before ducking in through a door. As Katz entered, the Libyan let the AK-74 drop from his hand and snatched for the 9 mm Browning tucked in the top of his pants. He had barely closed his fingers over the butt when Katz turned his Uzi loose. A scalding burst of pain erupted in the Libyan's stomach. He felt numb, as if he had been punched violently. He stumbled back, glancing down at his stomach, and saw the pulsing streams of red issuing from the holes in his body. Then Katz's second blast hit him. Higher up this time, stitching a ragged line of holes up the torso and sending 9 mm slugs coring deep into his chest. Two of those slugs ripped through the Libyan's heart, destroying the vital organ in seconds. He tumbled backward, falling over a chair, curling up in a ball as he hit the floor.

The whole of the warehouse seemed to have erupted with noise. Automatic weapons sent streams of bullets winging in crisscross patterns as the opposing groups strove to gain the upper hand. Any intention of negotiating verbally had long since been abandoned. Now every man in the building was struggling to stay alive.

Manning and Encizo, covering each other as they reloaded, were aware that Katz had become separated from them. Manning caught sight of the Israeli, still inside the office block. He also saw a couple of Libyans moving toward the offices. One signaled to the other, and they split apart, weapons rising as they neared the open doorway.

Manning didn't hesitate. He broke away from Encizo, snapping back the MP-5's bolt, tracking in on the closest of the Libyans. The Arab must have sensed Manning's approach, because he turned without warning, the muzzle of his AK-74 drawing down on Manning. The burly Canadian took the only action he could to evade the threat of the Soviet assault rifle. He took a full-length dive to the floor, rolling as he hit, absorbing the impact. He heard the crackle of the AK-74 and even felt the thud of the bullets biting against the concrete. Chips of the floor's surface flew in the air, some stinging the side of Manning's face. He kept moving, pulling his body around so that he could bring his SMG into play. Sooner or later the Libyan was going to get lucky and nail his target. Manning pushed his MP-5 out and up, catching the Libyan in his sight. He pulled the trigger and sent a hail of slugs at the target. A couple of them chewed a painful chunk out of the top of the Libyan's shoulder. It was a sharply painful wound, but not hard enough to put the guy down on the floor. Manning muttered to himself, set his sights again and fired a second time. The blast ripped the Libyan's throat out in a red flash. The guy staggered about, both hands clasped to his ruined throat, blood bubbling between his fingers. He slumped to his knees, eyes wide with fear. His shirtfront was rapidly drenched in bright blood.

The Libyan's partner turned in Manning's direction, snarling in defiance. He yanked the barrel of his AK-74 around, his finger tightening on the trigger.

Encizo released a long burst from his MP-5, catching the Libyan in the side. At the same moment, Katz stepped out of the office and opened fire with his Uzi, his lash of 9 mms ripping into the Libyan's back, shattering his spine. A finished man, the Arab crashed to the floor.

The Phoenix commandos and Giraud's team had the Libyans and their French allies caught between them. Though they must have sensed their dilemma, the opposition refused to yield. They returned fire with fire, and some of their bullets found a target. One of Giraud's men went down with a bullet-shattered left leg.

Two more Libyans were driven to the floor under a hail of bullets. One French gangster fell to his knees, his hands clutched to his bleeding torso. Another took a shot to the head from Giraud himself, sprawling full-length in his death throes.

Four Libyans remained. One, a powerfully built man with a thick, dark beard, seemed to be in authority. He yelled something to his men, and as one they turned and ran across the warehouse.

It quickly became apparent where they were heading.

Two cars were parked to one side. A Citroën and a Renault.

The bearded Libyan yanked open the Citroën's door and scrambled in. He fired the motor, flooring the gas pedal. He was yelling to the others to get in. With their weapons still blazing away, they pulled open the doors and threw themselves into the car.

Encizo got off a burst that caught a terrorist in the left shoulder and arm. The Libyan lost his grip on the car door as it lurched into movement, tires whining against the concrete. As the Citroën shot forward, the wounded man stumbled and fell.

One of Giraud's men made a valiant attempt to halt the accelerating car. He put himself in the path, leveling his MAT-49. Nothing happened when he pulled the trigger; whether it was a jam in the mechanism or he was simply out of ammunition, no one knew. The French policeman made a frantic attempt to rectify the fault, but he had left it too late.

The front of the speeding Citroën struck him and hurled his shattered body over the hood. The unfortunate man crashed to the warehouse floor, his legs twisted awkwardly beneath him.

The Citroën screeched out through the warehouse door and sped along the dock.

"No way they're getting off!" Manning yelled.

He ran to the other car and threw himself behind the wheel. The key was in the ignition. Manning turned it, the engine catching first time. Then the passenger door was flung open, and Rafael Encizo bounded into the seat beside the Canadian.

"You can't shoot and drive," he explained simply.

Manning knocked the Renault into gear and popped the clutch. The car erupted across the warehouse and out through the door.

By the time Manning cleared the warehouse entrance, the Citroën was midway along the dock, weaving recklessly around the stacks of goods and equipment dotted along the quayside.

"That guy is in one hell of a hurry," Manning said.

"To be honest," Encizo replied, "I'm not."

Up ahead, as the Citroën swerved around a stack of large fuel drums, its rear fender clipped one of the metal containers. The stack began to slide, and the heavy drums rolled out across the quay.

"*¡Dios!*" Encizo exclaimed.

His outburst was directed as much to the fact that Manning hadn't reduced his speed as to the threat of the tumbling fuel drums.

"Hang on!" the Canadian ordered.

He shoved his foot down hard, sending the Renault swinging toward the edge of the quayside. The Renault's wheels came to within an inch of the edge, with nothing to stop them going over into the water if Manning's timing was out. The Canadian grimly hung on to the wheel, keeping the car on a steady course. They shot clear of the cascading drums with inches to spare. Manning eased the wheel, putting the Renault back on course.

The Citroën roared on, heading straight for the dock gate. The security guard, already alerted by the shooting, had opened the gate in readiness for the police he had just summoned. The Citroën went through the gate flat out, with Manning pushing the Renault at a similarly reckless speed. The two cars shot up the access road, turning with squealing tires onto the dock road. The terrorist driver began to alter course frequently, hoping to lose Manning in the process. In close formation the two cars hurtled through the Marseilles streets.

There were few people about, and the streets were virtually deserted. The few passersby stared in amazement and anger at the spectacle of two cars racing through their city's streets. The anger turned to fear when one of the passengers in the lead car leaned out from a window and opened fire with an automatic rifle. The bullets were wide of their target, kicking up sparks when they hit the road surface. A couple of deflected slugs shattered a window in a corner bakery.

Soon they had left behind the city proper and were progressing through the outskirts. Despite the Citroën's maneuvering, Gary Manning kept on its tail, grimly determined to stay with the vehicle.

Without warning the Citroën took a sharp right, its rear end fishtailing wildly. For a few seconds the car rose on its right side, the wheels briefly losing contact with the road.

"That maniac is going to kill someone before he's finished," Encizo said. He hung on to his own seat as Manning wrestled with the Renault's wheel during their own high-speed turn around the corner.

The Citroën roared up the road that was leading in the direction of the hills surrounding Marseilles. Houses were not so much in evidence in the area. They were moving into open country, which meant less contact with innocent people.

Again the Citroën changed course, skidding onto a dusty track that veered cross-country. Dust billowed up from beneath its spinning wheels. Manning followed. The track was uneven, and the tires whomped into the deep ruts that marred its surface.

"Try and keep on a level course," Encizo asked as he attempted to reload the MP-5.

"These roads weren't built with smooth driving in mind," Manning replied, easing off the gas pedal.

Encizo managed to slot in a fresh magazine. He yanked back the cocking bolt. "Now you can open her up," he said.

"Great," the Canadian responded.

He tromped his foot down hard. The rocking car slewed around a sharp bend to the left. "There they are," Manning exclaimed.

The speeding vehicle came into sight. It was sliding from side to side as the driver chose speed over cautious driving.

"That car is just about ready to roll over," Manning said.

"Save us a job if he does," Encizo remarked cynically.

The Canadian maintained a steady course, keeping the Renault close on the Citroën's tail.

"Watch out!" Encizo yelled.

A man's head and shoulders appeared out of a rear window. An SMG was in his hands. Flame blossomed from the muzzle, the crackle of the weapon lost in the rush of wind from the speeding cars. Bullets clanged along the Renault's bodywork, though none penetrated.

The Citroën suddenly struck a deep rut. The front of the car dipped, then bounced out of the rut. The Citroën went briefly out of control and broadsided across the track. Despite his urgency to get away, the driver was forced to reduce speed, bringing his vehicle almost to a halt.

"Now we've got him," Encizo said.

Manning stepped on the brake, bringing the Renault to a shuddering halt. The Phoenix warriors exited the car, weapons up and ready.

The terrorists sent a burst of autofire their way, and Manning broke to the left, dropping to one knee and leveling the MP-5. He triggered a short burst, aiming for the Citroën's rear window. Glass imploded, showering the occupants. The Citroën stalled, then came to a dead stop.

The driver's door burst open, and a figure sprang out. It was the bearded Libyan. He hit the ground and rolled, coming up firing. He had a heavy automatic pistol in his hand. His first shot missed Encizo, but his second found its target. Encizo spun off balance as the slug ripped through his upper arm.

Manning saw Encizo take a hit, but couldn't go to his partner's aid immediately. The Citroën had disgorged its other two passengers. They had erupted from the rear of the car and were turning their AK-74s on Manning.

The 5.45 mm slugs chewed the ground just short of the Canadian. Manning didn't remain in the same position. He didn't want to give the Libyans the chance to range in on him.

Turning the MP-5 across his body, Manning triggered a burst in the direction of the Libyans. His shots were off target, but ripped into the rear of the Citroën. There was a sudden thump, and the rear of the Citroën lifted into the air and was consumed by flames as the gas tank blew. The concussion slammed into the Libyans, knocking them off their feet. Manning didn't give them a chance to recover. He pinned both Arabs to the ground with the MP-5's 9 mm hail of slugs, turning the dazed terrorists into dying terrorists as his slugs scythed through their flesh.

Sickened by the impact of the bullet coring through his arm, Encizo summoned every ounce of energy, focusing it on staying upright and fighting back. He knew he would only have fleeting seconds to respond. The bearded Libyan would not want to lose his advantage now.

The Cuban was right. The Libyan, seeing his bullet strike its target, grinned to himself. It was his turn, and he had the advantage. As the big automatic pistol ended its recoil, he began to swing it down toward its target, his finger already taking up the trigger's slack.

But with his weapon, Encizo had not needed to recover from a previous shot. All he had to do was jam the MP-5 against his hip and pull the trigger. Holding the trigger back, he allowed the full magazine to rip the muzzle in a continuous blast of sound. The Libyan was spun around by the lethal force of the shots. Unable to remain on his feet, he toppled to the ground in a red cloud.

Gary Manning dashed across to where Encizo stood, clutching his free hand to his bleeding arm.

"Let's see what we can do for that," the Canadian offered.

"Just wrap something round it for now. Then get me back to the others. Giraud will probably be able to organize some medical help."

"I hope he's got some information on where Karen might be," Manning said.

The Cuban glanced at his friend. He felt for Manning. It must have been hell having to carry on with the mission while all the time being worried about Karen Hoffe. He just hoped that any news they might get turned out to be good news.

15

The warehouse was a scene of high activity. Manning parked next to an ambulance with a flashing blue light on its roof. He climbed out as a uniformed police officer approached.

Manning explained that he was working with Giraud and asked to be taken to him.

The undercover officer was standing in the middle of the warehouse together with Phoenix Force.

"You stop them?" Katz asked.

Manning nodded.

"We need some medical help for Cicero," he said. "He caught a bullet in the arm."

"Where is he?" Giraud asked.

"In the Renault parked just outside."

"I will see to it right away," Giraud promised.

After he had moved away, Manning turned to the Force. "You get any information from these creeps?"

"Nothing," James said.

"Great," Manning muttered. "That's real help."

"None of them were in any fit state to talk, Gary," Katz explained.

Giraud rejoined the group just then, and Manning turned to him. "Can't we get anything from this?" he asked. "Giraud, what have you found out?"

"Not a great deal. These men, the warehouse, all belong to one of the local crime-bosses. A man named Larousse. He runs one of the Marseilles mobs," Giraud explained.

"Perhaps he can tell us what we need to know," Katz said.

"The only thing we have learned is that the Libyans have something to hide," James pointed out.

"Whatever that is," Katz said, "it has gone. Right now it's somewhere out at sea."

"Sailing in international waters by now," Giraud added, "where I can't touch it."

"But we can," McCarter said. "Right, Kaplan?"

Katz nodded. "Right. But we have to deal with Testarov and his group first."

"We have to *find* them first," Manning remarked.

"Let's ask our neighborhood gangsters," volunteered McCarter. "They might know."

"You could be right," Katz said. "Ferney was the fixer in this setup. He gave Delgado the information Testarov fed him. The Libyans were accommodated by Larousse's organization, so there's a tie-up between them all. Someone, somewhere, must know where the KGB is based."

"I'd say our best bet would be one of Larousse's men," Manning offered. "The Libyans won't talk.

It would be a waste of time trying with them. We need answers now!''

"Why not go to the source?" James suggested.

McCarter picked up on the black warrior's thoughts. "Pay a visit to Larousse himself?" McCarter warmed to the idea. "Go in hard and pin the bugger to the wall before he knows what's hit him."

"Do you know where this guy hangs out?" Manning asked.

Giraud nodded. He suddenly grinned. "Larousse won't like it," he said.

"He isn't supposed to like it," Katz pointed out. "I think it's worth a try."

"As this is strictly unofficial," Giraud said, "I can't become physically involved. But there's nothing to stop me driving you to his place and waiting outside with the engine running."

"Tell me about Larousse," Katz said.

"A hard man," Giraud began, "but clever. We've never made anything stick. He had very good lawyers and also friends in high places—enough said? Larousse has establishments all over Marseilles. He's into prostitution, smuggling, gambling. He'll deal in anything if it means money for him at the end. Extortion. Gun running. You name it, Larousse has done it."

"What about drugs?" James asked.

"One of his expanding sidelines. Growing in a big way. Larousse has it sewn up. He imports the stuff and distributes it through his own organization. Sells it through his restaurants and clubs. Peddles it on the streets, around the schools.''

"This scumbag needs a good shaking up," the Chicago hardass said bitterly. Of all the criminal types Phoenix Force had to deal with, drug peddlers were the ones who got Calvin James really going. He'd had personal experience of the misery drugs could bring. His own sister had died from an overdose. Now James came down with a heavy hand on anyone he found handling the deadly narcotics that could ruin and destroy so many lives.

"Would our timing be right?" McCarter asked. "To go to Larousse's place now?"

At Giraud's approving nod, Katz clapped him on the shoulders. "Good," Katz said. "Let's do it."

Making certain they were fully armed, the Force accompanied Giraud outside. While the officer went to speak to one of his people, Katz led the Phoenix team to the ambulance in which Encizo was being treated.

"The things people will do just to get off doing a job of work," McCarter remarked with a grin. "How are you, chum?"

"A little sore," Encizo answered.

"How bad is the wound?" James asked, casting an interested eye over the ambulance's medical facilities.

"The bullet went right through," the Cuban said.

"Rest up a while," Katz told him. "We have to attend to some business, so we will see you later."

Encizo failed to hide his disappointment. He did, however realize that as a wounded member of the team, he could not contribute fully.

"What's the layout of this place you're taking us to?" Manning asked as Giraud led them to his car.

"Larousse lives over one of his restaurants on the Quai de Rive-Neuve, on the Old Port."

On that street were many of the bouillabaisse speciality restaurants. But because of heavy tourism, many of them were dubious establishments where the only specialty was the spiel of the hucksters on the street who spent their time trying to persuade the unwary into a restaurant. Many a tourist fell for the patter, ate the so-called bouillabaisse and suffered for it later. But there was no point in going back to complain. The restaurants had their own way of dealing with dissatisfied customers.

Giraud drove slowly along the dock, crowded now with police cars and emergency vehicles. They passed through the gate and back toward the city.

"Like many of these hard-line racketeers, Larousse is a very basic man. He understands the rule of the hard hand and the gun. He is extremely wealthy. Has the money to buy anything he wants, to live where he chooses. Instead he lives over his grubby restaurant, in the same area where he was born. He wields a lot of power and he's respected because of that power. No one steps out of line with him."

"First time for everything," McCarter said breezily.

Giraud glanced at the Briton through the rear-view mirror. "Is he always like this?" he asked.

"Yeah," James replied. "We imagine it must have been something that happened during his childhood. Some trauma that's left him with antisocial tendencies."

The Frenchman shook his head. He looked across at Katz, who was sitting beside him in the front of the car. "I do not envy you having to command this bunch."

"It could be worse," The Israeli said lightly.

"How so?"

"Harper being a twin."

"Not a thought I'd like to go to bed with," James said.

Giraud chuckled to himself. They were all mad, he decided. But in their line of work, a little madness probably helped.

They reached their destination a short time later. Giraud cruised slowly along the street.

"That's the one," he said as he drove by the restaurant owned by Larousse. "The Fish Bowl. Not what you would call a very classy name, but Larousse is not a classy guy."

He eased the car to a stop a couple of hundred yards farther along the street. "I will turn around and wait for you. I don't want to know what you intend doing in there. Just do it well."

As the Force climbed out of the car, Katz asked, "Does Larousse speak English?"

"He speaks it very well. Also German and Spanish. Even a little Arabic. Larousse does business with an international clientele, so he makes certain he understands their language. Just in case they try to trick him."

"Speaks well of the man," Katz remarked. "It means he's no fool."

The Phoenix warriors crossed the street and made their way to the restaurant. Giraud had told them that there was a side entrance to the place, down a narrow entry beside the building. It was closed off from the street by a wooden door.

"Do we use the easy way or the hard?" McCarter asked.

"No time for niceties," Katz answered.

McCarter put his shoulder to the gate and pushed, testing the resistance. The wood, long-since dried by the hot climate, was brittle. It gave under pressure. The tough Briton drew back, then drove his full weight against the door. It gave with a sharp crack, tearing the lock from the frame.

"Last one in is a sissy," McCarter said, pushing his way through.

There was a walled-in area beyond the gate, with a shed and a garage. A patio held lounge chairs and an outdoor table with a large umbrella.

As McCarter strode swiftly along the path running alongside the main building, a door opened. A man stepped out. He was peering around with sleepy eyes. He had his pants on but was shoeless, and his shirt hung open. There was an Ingram MAC-10 in his hand. He was muttering to himself, obviously annoyed at being woken.

The Cockney swiftly increased his pace and reached the man before he could collect his thoughts. The guy glanced around as McCarter's shadow fell across him. He made a slow-motion attempt to lift the MAC-10, but McCarter's right fist walloped him across the side of his jaw. The sound of the blow rang sharp and clear in the still air. The impact spun the man around and bounced him into the wall. Before he could even think of defending himself, McCarter hit him again with quick sledging punches that put the man down hard.

Katz put up a hand to make them all pause. They listened, but only silence greeted them. Apparently no one else had been disturbed.

McCarter took the fallen Ingram and unloaded it, then tossed the magazine underneath a tub of flowers standing against the wall.

Katz motioned them on, and they entered through the open door. They were in the kitchen. It smelled of garlic and onions, with an underlying odor of fish. A pot of coffee steamed on the stove, and on a table a small radio played softly.

Katz led the way through to the passage beyond. An open arch led through to the restaurant. On the opposite side of the passage other doors led to a lounge furnished with heavy, dark pieces, and a large dining room. Both were empty.

They moved on and reached the stairs. After a smooth ascent, they saw a number of doors at the top.

"Time to do your stuff," James said to Mc-Carter.

The Briton moved to the first door, smashing it open with his foot. As the door crashed open, Manning went in, his MP-5 tracking the room ahead of him. It was an empty bedroom.

Aware that they may have alerted the occupants in other rooms, the Force moved quickly. Another bedroom, occupied by a man and a woman, was next. The guy rolled out of bed, grabbing for the autopistol on the chair beside him. James, who had entered the room, took him out of commission with a hard kick to the jaw that sent him into the arms of his female companion. She stared at the black warrior, her jaw dropping open in stunned silence.

"Just stay calm," James said in French.

"What do you want?" she asked, clutching the sheet to herself.

James pointed the MP-5's muzzle at the unconscious hood and asked, "Is he Larousse?"

The woman shook her head. "The next room," she volunteered.

"Be sure you're telling me right," James snapped.

Manning, standing in the doorway, called over his shoulder. "Larousse is next door."

"Go for it," McCarter yelled to Katz. The Briton hit the door with his foot, smashing it open.

Katz went in low, his Uzi braced against his metal prosthesis.

The bedroom was no better furnished than any of the other rooms. It contained furniture that had clearly seen better days. Once richly colored, the carpet had faded and was worn in some areas. Against the far wall was a large double bed, and as Katz burst into the room, the occupant was already out of bed and on his feet.

The man was big, a large-boned fellow with a broad weathered face and cold, empty eyes. He was clad in striped pajamas. There was a .45-caliber Colt Automatic in one large fist. It swept around as Katz appeared, then exploded with sound. The heavy slug whacked into the door frame, ripping a large chunk of wood free.

Katz hit the floor. It was a reflex action. Pure survival instinct that allowed the Israeli to respond faster than he might have done under normal circumstances.

The Phoenix commander rolled, gathering his feet under him, and lunged up off the floor in a continuous movement. He sprang forward, slashing the metal hooks of his prosthesis at the man with the smoking .45. The steel prongs caught the weapon and smashed it from the guy's hand. Before the autopistol had hit the floor, Katz struck out again, this time with his Uzi. The metal body of the SMG crunched against the underside of the big man's jaw, snapping it shut. Blood burst from the taut lips, spilling down the front of the pajamas. Uttering a groan, the big man dazedly stumbled back and lost his balance. He fell, jarring the room as he crashed to the floor.

Katz was on him in an instant, jabbing the muzzle of the Uzi into the soft flesh of the man's throat.

"You want to live? Or do you want to die?" the Israeli snapped harshly. "Make your choice. Now!"

McCarter had already followed Katz into the room. He knelt beside the Israeli and emphasized Katz's demand by placing the barrel of the Walther P-88 to the side of the prisoner's skull.

The man held up a hand, waving it urgently as he tried to catch his breath. "Wait," he gasped. "What . . . what do you want?"

"You, Larousse," Katz stated, rapping out his words.

"So you have me. What are you going to do? Kill me?"

"Perhaps," Katz said. "Your life is of no consequence to us."

"Then tell me what it is you want?" the gangster said, spitting blood from his mouth.

"An address," Katz said.

"Who for?"

"The Russians and their Libyan friends. Nothing more. Just tell me where they are."

"Do it fast, friend," Manning said, adding his weapon to those already threatening Larousse. "Don't mess with us. We aren't your local scum. You cheap gangsters may figure you're tough, but in our world you wouldn't last five minutes. Now answer the man, or I'll blow your head off myself."

There must have been something in Manning's voice that convinced Larousse he was in a potentially fatal position. It may have been the hard gleam in the Canadian's eyes or the white knuckles of the hand holding the MP-5. Whatever it was, it worked. The Marseilles hood nodded weakly, and when he was given more breathing room, he wiped at his aching jaw with his sleeve.

"There is a villa located some eight miles out of Marseilles, in the hills overlooking the city. Take the road leading north and follow the signs for Aix-en-Provence. After a few miles you will come upon a narrow road leading up into the hills. It will indicate a small village—Ligren. Through the village, follow the road on up into the hills and you will see the villa standing on a limestone bluff. It has a high stone wall all around it."

"Who owns the villa?" Katz asked.

"I do," Larousse answered.

"Just one more question," Katz said. "Where has the Libyan ship gone?"

"I don't know. Kill me if you don't believe me, but they would tell no one where they were bound."

Katz glanced at the others. They all sensed that Larousse was telling them the truth. The gangster was too scared to lie.

"Tie them all up," the Israeli ordered. "Bring up the one we found downstairs."

The occupants of the house were herded into Larousse's bedroom. McCarter produced some lengths of rope he had found in the garage. Once the prisoners had all been securely trussed up, the Force left the room, closing the door behind them.

They filed out of the house, concealing their weapons under their coats, and returned to the street via the side gate. As he had promised, Giraud was waiting for them some yards along the street. Phoenix Force climbed into the police undercover car and Giraud pulled away from the curb.

"How did it go?" he asked.

"Fine," Katz told him. "We got what we wanted. The Russians are in a villa in the hills overlooking Marseilles. The villa belongs to Larousse."

"How did you get him to talk?"

"Friendly persuasion," Manning responded.

"It might help if you could arrange for Larousse and his people to be kept on ice for a few hours," Katz suggested. "We don't want them getting to a telephone and warning our Russian friends."

"No problem," Giraud assented. "I'll send a couple of squad cars along to the restaurant on the pretext of the recent disturbance. Larousse and his people will be taken to a station house for questioning. We can keep them off the streets for a couple of days if need be."

He reached for the hand microphone under the dash and contacted the police dispatch department. He quickly outlined what he wanted, and was told that the squad cars would be at the scene within minutes.

"Where to now?" Giraud asked.

"Our hotel," Katz said. "We need some time to get ourselves together before we go after the Soviets. Strategy must be considered, and I think we could use a brief rest, along with a meal and a weapons check."

"The hotel it is," Giraud said, "and in the meantime, I'll see what I can do about locating that Libyan ship. We may also get a lead from the prisoners taken at the dock. If I get anything that may be of interest, I will pass it along."

"Be nice to get back to the hotel," McCarter remarked. "Hey, anybody know the French for a can of Coke and a steak?"

16

"It appears that we have been caught napping again," Leoni Testarov said, watching for Reiger's reaction.

"I've just heard," the German agent said.

No more than a half hour earlier, the KGB man had received a telephone call from a paid informant about the firefight at the docks. The informant was a legacy from Ferney. The man had connections in the Marseilles police, and the information had come firsthand from one of the officers called to the docks after the gun battle.

"At least Rashid had the good sense to leave earlier than originally planned," Reiger said. "If the ship had still been tied up at the quay, it would have all been over for them."

"I'm beginning to think we should have done the same, Peter," Testarov said. "We should have gone after them directly. I was wrong to sit back and wait. Since they arrived in Marseilles, our American team has been extremely busy. They appear to be cutting their way through everything in their path. What next? A visit here?"

"That could happen," Reiger admitted. "If they get the location of the villa, I wouldn't be at all surprised. These men have a knack for being in the right place at the right time."

"Then perhaps we may yet eliminate them," Testarov said. "If we can get them out here, where we are in control."

"There was a similar situation in Germany," Reiger pointed out. "And they overcame that one."

"The difference being that we are going to be waiting for them," Testarov explained. "We work on the assumption that they are coming. So we stay prepared."

"We have armed guards on the inside," Reiger said. "What about a couple outside the grounds? Placed in concealment thirty yards from the perimeter wall, and supplied with radios. It would also give us the advantage of having someone out there at the Americans' backs. We could catch them in a cross fire."

"Yes, that's a good idea," Testarov said. "We'll have Kochak in. Get him to pick a couple of men who are good at sniping."

"What do you intend to do with the woman?" Reiger asked.

"Once her duty as a lure has been achieved, we kill her," Testarov said without a moment's hesitation. "We cannot afford to have witnesses on the loose, can we, Peter? Or have you taken a fancy to her?"

"It wouldn't be hard to do," Reiger admitted. "She is very attractive, after all."

"I don't deny that," the KGB man said. "But there is a time and place for that kind of activity. During a mission is not that time or place."

"I hadn't forgotten," Reiger said, a thin smile on his lips.

"While we're adding to our defences, let's step up the interior patrols," Testarov said. "The more I think about it, the more I'm certain the Americans are going to come here. This time I intend to take them out. *Permanently.*"

17

At the hotel, the members of Phoenix Force found a number of surprises waiting for them.

The main one was that Rafael Encizo was there. Though his arm was bandaged and in a sling, the injury hadn't stopped him from making a telephone call through to Stony Man, apprising them of the current situation and also requesting information on the Libyan ship. Encizo had obtained the name of the vessel from one of the French police officers. He was waiting for Kurtzman to call back.

In the room, along with Encizo, were the team's aluminum weapons cases. They had been flown in by the U.S. government, with the permission of the French authorities, and had been delivered to the hotel.

"Now there's a sight for sore eyes," McCarter said, giving a case a pat.

"First let's get some food ordered," Katz suggested. "We'll make our plans while we eat. After that a couple of hours' sleep. And that goes for everyone," he added, fixing Manning with a stern look.

"Yeah, okay," the Canadian agreed. "I get the message."

"I don't mean to be hard on you, Gary," Katz said. "But we have to function as a team, or we're no use to each other."

"Hey, we'll get Karen back, mate," McCarter said.

Manning picked up the telephone and contacted room service. It took him a little time to persuade the woman who answered that the coffee and sandwiches were urgent. He even managed to put in an order for some cans of Coke for McCarter.

While they waited for the food, the Force unpacked the arms cases and systematically checked and rechecked every weapon. Magazines were loaded, spares added.

The Phoenix commandos were glad to have their own weapons back again. Though they were fully conversant with other arms, they felt distinctly more comfortable with their usual weapons. Their battlefield experience had shown them that in the heat of the firefight, when a delay of a second can mean the difference between life and death, an unfamiliar weapon can be fatal to its user.

McCarter for one was more than happy to have his Browning Hi-Power back. He had used the 9 mm autopistol for longer than he could recall. It had become an extension of his arm. When he held and used the Browning, it was like pointing his own finger. He did it without conscious thought. It was a little different as far as his SMG was concerned. Due to a couple of instances when his previous weapon—an Ingram MAC-10—had let him down, placing him in potential danger, the Briton had reluctantly abandoned the auto weapon. His final choice of a new arm had been the Intertec KG-99. McCarter had been using it for a while already and was getting used to the SMG's performance. He still hankered for his Ingram and had used it on a couple of missions since his changeover to the KG-99.

Katz had his Uzi SMG, along with the SIG-Sauer P-226 handgun that had seen him through countless confrontations. The SA-80, Manning's second piece of main hardware, was a weapon the Canadian was getting to grips with. He was becoming comfortably familiar with its bull-pup configuration and the SUSAT sight that allowed good target acquisition in day or night conditions. As far as his handgun was concerned, Manning persevered with the Walther P-5 9 mm autopistol, though if truth were told, he did prefer the .357 Desert Eagle. The Beretta 92-SB had quickly found favor with Calvin James. The former SEAL found no problems adjusting to the new handgun. He might have caused a fuss if someone had suggested he swap his M-16 for something else. The combat rifle was too versatile a weapon to abandon. With its high performance as an assault rifle, the M-16 also boasted the M-203 grenade launcher, which could turn it into a deadly piece of equipment.

Besides their sidearms and SMGs, the Phoenix warriors took along fragmentation and concussion grenades, plus numerous other items. Each man also carried a combat knife of his own preference.

When the refreshments arrived, Manning and James collected them at the door, tipping the young waitress well. That served to pleasantly distract her, and she went away happy and not terribly curious why she had been kept out of the room.

Clearing some space, the Phoenix team attacked the sandwiches and the coffee. They pushed aside thoughts of what lay ahead, allowing themselves some time for relaxation.

"After this we get a couple of hours' sleep," Katz said firmly. "That means everyone."

Encizo, who knew he wouldn't be going along, drew Katz aside after the meal. "I'll stay by the phone," he said. "I want to be there when Stony Man calls back. I get worried just thinking about those Libyans out there on that ship. What the hell are they up to, Katz?"

"I wish I knew," the Israeli replied. "It has to mean trouble for someone. The Libyans have spent too much time and trouble on whatever plan they've devised. Stick close to that phone, Rafael. Giraud may also be contacting us with whatever he may have come up with."

"Leave that to me," the Cuban said. "I'll stand by while you catch some shut-eye."

18

The villa stood on a section of high ground that afforded an excellent view of the surrounding countryside. High stone walls protected the building and its grounds. Outside the walls the terrain was heavily overgrown with tangled foliage and thick grass. A curving track of hard-packed earth ran for half a mile from the public road to terminate at tall wrought-iron gates.

Phoenix Force was concealed in a dense thicket a quarter mile from the villa. They had parked their car off the road, well camouflaged by foliage so there would be little chance of the sun reflecting on the windows and giving their position away. They had been making their approach when, at the word from Katz, Manning had pulled off the road and into the undergrowth.

They sat in silence and studied the terrain surrounding the villa.

"A couple of men armed with rifles and concealed out beyond the walls could move in on us from behind once they had let us pass," the Israeli said. "I'd bet on it."

"Makes sense," James admitted.

"Okay, I'll check it out," Manning suggested. He pulled a pair of powerful binoculars from his weapons bag and climbed out of the car. He selected a high spot and bellied down in the deep grass. Settling into a comfortable position, he embarked on a painstaking surveillance of the terrain surrounding the villa. The others, knowing it could take considerable time, began to change into their combat gear.

It was midday. The hills were framed by a sharp cloudless blue sky. The heat, though partially relieved by a fitful breeze blowing inland from the ocean, seemed to make time stand still.

A quarter hour passed, then thirty minutes. Despite the lengthy wait, the Phoenix warriors sat patiently. It didn't matter how long they waited. Before they moved on the villa, they had to be certain nothing had been overlooked: there were no second chances after a fatal error.

Manning suddenly raised his hand, one finger extended to indicate that he had located someone. When Katz moved up beside him, Manning pointed out the concealed sentry.

It took another fifteen minutes to spot the second man. The Canadian then spent another twenty minutes rechecking in case he had overlooked anyone. Finally satisfied, he returned to the car. After changing into his combat gear, he removed a long gun-case from the car and opened it. Inside was the special rifle Manning had decided to bring along for just such a need. It was the Anschutz, a precision-built ultrapowerful air rifle, which fired Thorazine-loaded hypnodarts. A hit from one of the darts would put a man to sleep in seconds. The Anschutz provided an ideal method for taking out opponents swiftly and silently. It was also equipped with a Bushnell scope, making it an extremely accurate, long-distance weapon.

With the rifle loaded, Manning moved back to his observation point. He stretched out and raised the Anschutz to his shoulder to peer through the scope at the nearest target. He adjusted the Bushnell for range, then resighted. When he fired, he was able to observe the result through the scope. The distant sentry, who was in a shallow depression, sat upright suddenly. His head turned sharply as if he was looking for the source of the stinging at the back of his neck. A moment later he slumped forward, sinking facedown in the grass. Changing his position, Manning tracked in on the second guy. He was farther away. Manning took a long time settling his aim, adjusting for distance and the breeze factor. He eventually eased back the trigger. The Anschutz barely made a sound. The Canadian sharpshooter watched the target go down seconds after the hypnodart had struck home.

"All clear," he stated on his return to the car. He packed away the Anschutz and picked up his SA-80.

Katz quietly voiced his approval before he proceeded with the rundown of the assault plan. "David, you're with me," he said. "Cal, I'd like you and

Gary to handle the front gate. You'll probably have to put a HE grenade through it. David and I will get in by the back way."

"How are we handling this?" James asked.

"With extreme prejudice," Katz replied. "These people have wantonly murdered American citizens and people working for the U.S. simply to gain attention. They warrant no mercy in this instance. Our job is to stop them for good. They wanted a face-to-face with us—so we'll give them one. Phoenix style. One other priority. Karen may be in there. We want her out unharmed if possible."

"Thanks, Katz," Manning said.

"Oh, God, I think he's going to cry again," McCarter muttered.

"Let's set our watches," Katz instructed, and when they had, he said, "We hit in precisely thirty minutes, gentlemen, so don't be late."

The force split into the assigned groups. With final nods and words of encouragement, they moved away from the car and were soon swallowed up by the thick foliage.

KATZ AND MCCARTER had reached the high wall surrounding the villa. McCarter handed his KG-99 to Katz. He estimated the height of the wall, took a few steps back and made a short run. His powerful legs thrust him upward while his hands reached for the top of the wall. McCarter got a grip, took a deep breath, then hauled himself up. He swung one leg over the top, quickly dragging himself onto the wide wall. He reached down and took the weapons Katz held up to him. Then he stretched his right arm down the wall and gripped the Israeli's wrist to haul him bodily up to the top.

The pair lay atop the wall, surveying the layout of the villa and its extensive grounds. There was a stand of timber near the wall they were lying on, with a dense garden spreading out from it. As Katz and McCarter scanned the area, they both realized that for defence purposes, leaving the trees had been a mistake. They formed a barrier between the villa and the boundary wall that gave all the advantage to an intruder. The trees should have been removed to allow a clear, unobstructed field of vision.

"If I ever meet the guy who landscaped this place," McCarter said, "I'll buy him a drink."

"Testarov will have made allowances for this blind spot," Katz pointed out. "Let's check it out."

They remained still and silent on the top of the wall. Watching and waiting. In the end their vigilance was rewarded. A burly, red-faced Russian, sweating in the heat, came tramping through the undergrowth. He carried an AK-74 in one hand and a walkie-talkie in the other. He made a slow, thorough inspection of the area, passing directly below the spot where Katz and McCarter lay.

The Phoenix warriors watched him move on along the base of the wall until he came to the edge of the trees. Once clear of the timber, the Russian moved off across the grounds.

"Okay, David, let's go," Katz said.

They swung down from the top of the wall, dropping to the soft, grassy earth below, then swiftly lost themselves in the shadow of the trees.

McCarter studied the grounds. Bigger than they had figured. Apart from the expansive garden, there was a tennis court surrounded by high wire-mesh. Nearer the villa itself was a large swimming pool.

He was about to speak when Katz made a sharp cutting motion with his hand.

Some distance away another armed figure had appeared. The hair above the man's broad Slavic face was cropped, and he toted a Franchi SPAS-12 combat shotgun. He was moving into the stand of trees, his line of travel bringing him on course for a confrontation with the Phoenix pair.

Katz caught McCarter's eye and made a cutting motion across his throat. The Brit nodded. He placed his KG-99 on the ground and unsheathed the Gerber Predator.

The KGB man tramped steadily through the trees. He wasn't just out for a stroll. His eyes were everywhere, peering, seeking, probing. It was obvious that Testarov had his people on full alert.

The Russian was only feet away. Despite the excellent camouflage they were wearing, both Katz and McCarter knew that the Soviet would spot them in a few seconds. Once that happened and the alarm was raised, the advantage surprise would bring them would be instantly lost.

McCarter moved quickly and efficiently. He simply rose out of the shadows at ground level, the Gerber glittering in his hand. He struck once, the keen blade of the knife plunging deep into the Russian's chest and penetrating his heart. Kicking the guy's legs from under him, McCarter followed him to the ground. He threw his body across the Russian's and clamped his free hand over his mouth to silence any outcry. He remained in position for a couple of minutes and only drew away when the Russian had ceased all movement. McCarter withdrew the Predator, poking the blade into the earth to clean off the blood.

Katz moved quickly to his side, handing the KG-99 back to the Cockney. A glance at their watches told them that the numbers were dropping away quickly. Too quickly.

The Israeli jerked his head toward the villa as a reminder that they needed to be closer to the house.

McCarter snatched up the dead Russian's shotgun and slung it across his shoulder.

The Brit was following hard on Katz's heels as they cut across the garden, heading in the general direction of the rear of the villa.

They had only traveled a few yards when they heard the dull explosion of Calvin James's first HE round. If matters had gone according to the plan, McCarter and Katz should have been at the rear of the villa.

As it was, fate had already pushed one in from left field, slowing McCarter and Katz down by a few minutes—minutes they could ill afford.

The sound of the explosion warned everyone in the vicinity.

The crackle of autofire reached the ears of the Phoenix pair. To the left of McCarter the earth was shredded by a line of 5.45 mm slugs. The shots came from the AK-74 of the first Russian the Phoenix warriors had seen while they were still on top of the wall.

McCarter skidded to a halt and spun around to face the enemy. Catching the sweating guard in the act of aiming again, McCarter didn't waste time. He leveled the KG-99 and triggered a long burst at the Russian. The first slugs missed, but they gave McCarter a chance to reassess range and trajectory. He eased the muzzle of the SMG up a fraction. The Russian's finger had just touched the trigger when McCarter's 9 mm slugs started to climb up his body. The first caught his hip, then he was rapidly stitched across the stomach and chest. The KGB man twitched spasmodically, and his AK-74 began to pump bullets into the sky. It was only after a few blank seconds that the guy realized he was lying flat on his back on the ground. His blood was pumping from his body in steady streams. The AK-74 slipped from his limp fingers, dead and silent like its owner.

McCarter took off after Katz, who was moving with surprising speed and agility. As Katz rounded the wire enclosing the tennis court, he caught sight of armed figures dashing across the patio area near the swimming pool.

"Watch yourself, David," the Israeli called.

"I see the buggers," McCarter replied.

One of the KGB men arced his AK-74 in Katz's direction, spraying flesh-seeking slugs at the target, but Katz wasn't there.

He had veered to one side, then dropped to the ground in a shoulder roll that took him yards away from the Russian's burst. Rising on one knee, Katz triggered the Uzi, sending a stream of 9 mm slugs into the surprised KGB man's torso.

Seeing one of their comrades go down brought out the worst in the Russians. They opened fire, raking the area with streams of deadly slugs.

McCarter jumped into the firefight with a vengeance. He opened up with his KG-99, taking out two of the Russians with his first burst. He caught them on the wide steps that led from the patio area to the tiled pool. The lead guy took a half-dozen slugs in his lower body. He collapsed helplessly, yelling as his body slithered ungraciously down the steps. He left a smear of blood on the pale stone of the steps. The second KGB man tried to avoid his downed companion, and while his attention was briefly held by the sight of his dying comrade, he felt a series of hard blows to his chest. He wasn't sure what had caused them for the first few seconds. But then he felt the deeper pain as the 9 mm slugs from McCarter's KG-99 drove deep into his body, shredding lungs and tearing his heart apart.

Katz reached the swimming pool and found himself trading shots with one of the Russians who had decided to fight from the far side of the pool. The

Russian kicked over a poolside table and dived for cover behind it. Katz shook his head, wondering what had given the Russian the idea that a flimsy table constructed of man-made materials would stop bullets.

He aimed the Uzi at the table and opened fire, emptying his magazine in a continuous burst. The sustained blast shattered the tabletop, the force of the slugs driving shards of plastic into the Russian's face and body. The Russian agent dropped his AK-74, lurching to his feet, pawing at his ruined face. Katz slid home a fresh magazine, cocked the Uzi and hit the Russian with a short burst to the chest. The guy staggered a few steps before plunging into the tranquil water of the pool.

McCarter reached the patio steps. As he did, he caught a flicker of movement inside an open door leading to an extension of the main villa building.

"Watch the door," the Cockney yelled to Katz as he saw armed men burst from the door and fan out across the wide patio.

Katz opened fire, cutting one running man down with his first salvo. McCarter, aware that his KG-99 must be almost exhausted, changed to the SPAS-12. He turned the captured weapon on the Russians spread out across the patio. The combat shotgun blasted its deadly load at the closest KGB man. The impact swept the guy off his feet and slammed him facedown on the patio, his body bleeding profusely from a dozen places. The SPAS erupted four more times before it clicked on an empty chamber. Three of those shots found targets, turning living men into bloody mush, flesh torn and bone shattered. The patio was streaked with blood.

The last Russian turned his AK-74 on Katz, certain that he had the edge on the invader. He was wrong. Even as his finger touched the AK's trigger, he felt a hot burst of pain stitch across his middle. The impact behind the blow took his breath, knocking him back a step. It happened so fast that the Russian still carried through his attempt to fire his own weapon. Then he became aware of a spreading of the pain. It erupted wildly, ripping through his body to envelop him. Only then did he realize fully that he had been shot. His limbs weakened and he fell, his body spurting blood across the smooth stone slabs of the patio.

With the patio clear, Katz and McCarter left the killzone and burst into the villa itself.

LOOKING AT HIS WATCH as the second hand swept away the final seconds, Manning tapped James on the shoulder. The black Phoenix warrior settled the M-16 against his shoulder and touched the trigger, sending an M-406 HE round at the villa's main gates. The grenade, designed to explode on impact, struck the gates and detonated with a crash. As the smoke from the explosion cleared, the Phoenix pair saw that the iron gates had been blasted open.

"Here we go," Manning said.

The Stony Man commandos ran for the gate, eyes searching for any movement. One KGB man was on the ground, his body bloody from the effects of being caught by the grenade blast. Farther along the drive a disoriented man was shaking his head, dazed by the concussion of the explosion.

As Manning breached the gate, he brought up the SA-80, triggering a burst at the dazed Russian. The KGB agent crashed to the ground, his AK-74 flying from nerveless fingers.

Ahead of Manning and James, the drive curved up to the front of the villa. There were three cars parked on the circular area near the front doors. Lawns flanked the drive, curving around the sides of the sprawling white-and-red building.

A babble of raised voices rang out, preceding the armed men who appeared from around the side of the villa, off to the left of the Phoenix warriors.

AK-74s stuttered out their angry sound, and bullets gouged the lawn, tearing up the carefully tended grass.

Calvin James swiveled in the direction of the advancing KGB men. A short exchange, supported by Manning, left two of them dead.

From the rear of the villa came the sound of autofire, indicating that Katz and McCarter had joined the fray.

Manning tracked in on the remaining KGB man and beat him to the trigger. The 5.56 mm slugs crashed into the Russian's torso, taking the Soviet killer out of the firefight for good.

And it was just in time, because an armed figure appeared on the far side of the parked cars. Resting his weapon across the hood of a gleaming Mercedes sedan, he started pumping shots at the Stony Man commandos.

Manning and James separated, hitting the ground in long dives.

The Canadian raked the Mercedes with 5.56 mm slugs, shattering windows and puncturing the steel body, driving the Russian sniper back for a few seconds.

It bought James the time he needed to load a fresh round into the grenade launcher of his M-16. Aiming quickly, the black warrior planted the HE round against the side of the Mercedes. It blew, rocking the big car, and filled the air with slivers of steel and glass. The KGB man, catching splinters that gouged the side of his face, pulled away from the car. He threw ill-aimed shots at the Phoenix pair as he attempted to find fresh cover.

Gary Manning had been waiting for his chance. The moment he had a clear shot, he put a stream of 5.56 mm slugs into the Soviet's body, slamming him back against the wall of the villa. The KGB man slithered along the wall and pitched facedown on the gravel.

James pulled a concussion grenade from his belt and yanked out the pin. He held the grenade in his right hand as he sprinted toward the villa's front door. He was aware of Manning close behind, covering his move.

The black warrior went up the steps and tossed the grenade in through the partly open doors. The concussion grenade exploded with a dull thump.

Manning kicked the doors open and stormed inside, with James right behind. They were in a large entrance area, where a wide staircase curved in a half circle, leading to the upper floor.

One KGB man was slumped across the bottom step, his hands clasped to his head. An AK-74 lay on the floor at his feet. Manning moved across and kicked the weapon aside. He caught a handful of the Russian's hair and yanked his head back.

The KGB man stared at him. Tears streamed from his eyes from the blast of the stun grenade.

"Where is the woman?" Manning snapped.

The man shook his head uncomprehendingly.

"Damn!" Manning cursed. "The woman," he repeated. "Hoffe. Karen Hoffe."

The name struck a chord with the Russian. He still didn't speak, but he waved a hand in the direction of the stairs.

McCarter and Katz burst through a door on the other side of the hall, having come through the villa without encountering any further opposition. It appeared that the main body of KGB men had been outside, covering the grounds.

"This guy says Karen is upstairs," Manning said.

"David, go with him," Katz ordered. "Cal, you stay with me. We haven't flushed them all out yet."

Manning and McCarter hit the stairs on the run. As they made their way to the top, McCarter saw two armed Soviets step into view.

"Gary, top of the stairs!" the Briton yelled.

He already had his KG-99 in motion, triggering the SMG the moment he lined up the nearest man. The weapon chattered, sending its load of 9 mm death winging through the air. The Russian twisted in agony as the slugs hammered his body. His light suit began to show the blood leaking from his punctured flesh. He toppled forward and bounced awkwardly down the stairs.

Manning had responded to McCarter's warning by dropping to a crouch and snap-aiming the SA-80 at the second Russian. The Canadian's shots ripped through the guy's upper body, striking the wall at his back. The KGB agent's death was swift and silent as he crumpled to the base of the wall.

Moving along the passage that led off from the head of the stairs, Manning and McCarter tensely surveyed the doors leading off.

Suddenly one of the doors opened, and the man they'd known as Martin Kohler using Karen Hoffe as a shield, moved into view. The German double agent had a pistol pressed to the side of Karen's head.

"Either put down your weapons, or she dies here and now," Reiger said flatly. "And don't believe I won't do it."

"I'm sure you will," Manning said.

"Then do it," Reiger snapped.

"No, Gary," Karen pleaded. "Don't listen to him."

"I brought you into this," Manning said. "I feel bad enough about that. I don't intend to get you killed, as well."

"You don't really think he's going to let me go?" Karen asked.

"I have to believe it."

"Enough talk," Reiger said. "Now throw down the weapons."

Manning exchanged looks with his partner. The Briton grinned.

"Step at a time," McCarter said softly, and placed his KG-99 on the floor.

After Manning had abandoned the SA-80, Reiger demanded, "Now the handguns."

"What name are you working under these days?" McCarter asked casually.

"My own. Peter Reiger."

Manning eased his Walther from its holster and tossed it to the floor.

Reiger glanced at McCarter. "And yours," he said.

The Cockney's face was expressionless as he slid the Browning from his shoulder holster.

From ground level there came a sudden outburst of gunfire and the crackle of autofire.

McCarter's gaze remained fixed on Reiger, and the Briton saw the man's eyes flicker uneasily before he swiveled for a brief moment in the direction of the stairs.

It was the reaction McCarter had been waiting for. The drooping barrel of the 9 mm Hi-Power rose, then steadied as McCarter locked on to his target.

Karen, who had been watching the Briton, was the first to realize his intention. She remained immobile, her attention held by the Browning's black muzzle.

Peter Reiger, his attention diverted for an instant by the gunfire downstairs, returned to his previous stance—and saw the Browning aimed at him.

No more than a second had passed, a mere flicker of time. But it was enough for Reiger to have lost his advantage and for McCarter to respond to the opening.

The Browning fired a single shot.

Reiger's finger was pressing the trigger of his automatic when the 9 mm slug struck him just above the right eye, penetrating his skull and coring into his brain. The German agent felt a stunning blow that overrode all other impressions. The world vanished in a blinding flash, and silence surrounded him. He was aware only of being snatched away from reality as his senses shut down. There was not even time for pain. Just a fleeting acceptance of defeat before eternal darkness reached out to swallow him.

As Reiger's limp form dropped to the floor, Karen ran to Manning. He stared at her for a moment, still trying to catch up with the swift turn of events.

"Hey, come on, you pair," McCarter said. "No time for all that romantic stuff now."

The unflappable Briton picked up Manning's weapons and thrust them into the Canadian's hands. Then he retrieved his KG-99.

Karen touched McCarter's hand. "Thank you," she said.

"If anything had happened to you, I would have had to put up with his miserable face for the rest of my life," the Cockney stated dryly. "Now, let's go and find the others."

"I WANT TESTAROV," Katz said firmly to Calvin James. "He's not getting away from me a second time."

"No way he's wriggling out of paying for murdering all those Americans," the black warrior agreed.

They moved across the hall, heading for the doors that led into the main section of the villa.

The doors opened before they reached them, and an armed KGB man stepped into view, opening up with the AK-74 he was carrying. A window behind James smashed as it was laced with 5.45 mm slugs. The KGB agent readjusted his aim, deciding to take out the black man first. James had strong views on that kind of thinking. He expressed them by triggering his M-16 and sending a stream of 5.56 mm messengers at the Soviet killer. The hail of bullets sent the gunman flying backward through the doorway.

James and Katz followed hard on the dead man's heels, storming the entryway and breaking to either side, low and moving fast.

The room was long, with a low ceiling. Sunlight streamed in through the large windows, bringing warmth to the brightly decorated room. Scatter rugs on the tiled floor added pools of color. The comfortable furniture contrasted with the polished wood beams and natural stone that had been incorporated in the design.

Two men were in the room. One was standing before the well-equipped bar, his bleak gaze fixed on the dead KGB man. He was Erik Kochak. His companion was facing the door, clutching a stubby Ingram in his hands. It was Leoni Testarov.

"Are these your terrifying specialists?" Kochak yelled as the Phoenix pair barreled into the room. "I'll take care of them myself!" The arrogant KGB major, still refusing to accept that Phoenix Force was something to be respected, swept his AK-74 off the bar top and searched for a target.

He became the target instead. Calvin James, rolling to his feet, leveled his M-16 and pulled the trigger, unleashing some sound American retribution at the KGB agent. Kochak caught a chestful of 5.56 mm slugs that hammered him back against the bar, his flesh shredded by the blast. The Soviet remained standing, blood frothing from his mouth, until James fired again, this time aiming a little higher and driving his shots into the heart. Kochak flopped forward to crash facedown on the tiled floor.

Katz had half-risen, coming face-to-face with Leoni Testarov. The KGB man caught the Israeli's eyes and held his glance for a long moment. There was no need for actual words. Both men recognized the other as an enemy, yet also as a professional.

That respect for the other's worth did not stop either of them from carrying out his duty.

It was simply a matter of whoever turned out to be the faster.

Ingram and Uzi filled the room with their noise.

Katz, recalling the previous encounter with Testarov, made certain that it was no mere wounding shot this time. He went for the head and the heart, arcing the Uzi's muzzle back and forth. Testarov collapsed, his upper body reduced to a sodden, pulpy mass by the devastating blast from the 9 mm SMG. The Ingram clattered across the tiles, nothing more lethal than smoke trailing from the muzzle.

"You okay?" James asked, clipping a fresh magazine into his M-16.

Katz nodded. He paused to take a final look at Testarov's body. "I am now," he replied.

They had three prisoners. The sentries Manning had put to sleep with his Anschutz and the KGB man from whom they'd learned Karen's whereabouts.

McCarter and James took one of the cars from the front of the villa and went to pick up the vehicle the Force had concealed. When they got back, the three Russians were placed in the back of another car. James drove, with McCarter beside him, his KG-99 trained on the sullen Soviets.

"Come on, fellers, don't be bad losers," McCarter said. "Look at it this way—at least you're all alive. And you've got a lot to look forward to once you get back home. A nice long vacation on the Gulag."

"Can't be bad, brothers," James grinned.

One of the Russians leaned forward, his face angry. He struggled to break the plastic riot cuffs binding his wrists.

"I am not your brother, black monkey," he snapped. "You are nothing."

"So you say," James answered, glancing over his shoulder. "But just remember one thing, man. You're the one trussed up like a damned turkey. And this black monkey and his buddies just went and kicked your Russian asses good and hard. Same goes for the next time, *tovarich*, and every time you try and play dirty."

"Come on, mate," McCarter said, "let's get these losers back to the safehouse. We've got a few questions to ask them."

19

Giraud found Phoenix Force a room at the safe-house where the prisoners could be questioned about the Libyans.

Manning, accompanied by Karen, took one of the cars and set off to pick up Encizo from the hotel.

In the assigned room Calvin James was readying one of the KGB agents for treatment with scopolamine, a drug used in extracting information from reluctant captives. He had examined all the Russians and found them to be in good health. One of the drawbacks of scopolamine was the possibility that it could harm anyone with a weak heart or allied medical problems. Satisfied that the Soviets were fit, James prepared the first of them for an injection.

While he was busying himself with the prisoners, Katz and McCarter had a meeting with Giraud, so that the French officer could relay the information he had gathered about the Libyan ship.

"The *Palomar* is a twenty-thousand ton freighter," Giraud informed them. "She was built in Korea eighteen years ago. Had a busy life for the first ten years, traveling the Pacific routes as part of a Greek-owned shipping line. Eight years back she was sold off as part of a cost-cutting program. A company based in Cyprus bought her. They put her on island-hopping freight runs around the Mediterranean. Three years ago the Cyprus company ran into financial trouble and put the *Palomar* up for sale. Her new owners were registered in Ireland. Shortly after the purchase she started regular runs in this area. General cargo carrying. Calling at ports in Spain, France, Italy. Up and down the coastline. Nothing spectacular. All bread-and-butter work.

"We did some more digging, but this is where the story becomes a little complicated. The Irish registration appears to be nothing more than a fronting organization for whoever the real owners are. We got lost in a tangle of subsidiary companies. One point did emerge. The cargoes that the *Palomar* has been carrying during the past couple of years could not have made much profit. In fact the ship has been operating at a loss. So that means she's been heavily subsidized. Someone has been covering her losses in order to keep her in business. The only answer we can come up with is that the *Palomar* is being used for other undeclared purposes. The kind you don't advertise."

"Could be anything from running guns to running dope," Katz said.

"Plenty of scope in this area for all kinds of dirty dealings," McCarter added. "Including terrorism."

Giraud nodded.

"A ship like the *Palomar*, regularly trading along the Mediterranean coastline, becomes part of the scenery. All the port authorities will know her. She would be in and out of a dozen ports."

"The old familiarity trick," McCarter said. "Everyone is so used to seeing her they don't give her a second look."

"And that would pay dividends if the *Palomar* was to be used as part of some covert operation," Katz observed. "So all we need to know is where she's going—and when she'll arrive."

"I'm trying to get some details on that now," Giraud said. "There should be some registration of her intended course. If it was properly logged before she left port."

"Even if it was logged," McCarter said, "what's to stop her changing once she gets out to sea?"

Giraud had to admit that was a possibility.

"What about the warehouse?" Katz asked. "Did you pick up any material evidence?"

"We brought away a number of bags of rubbish. A team is going through it now. Come and take a look for yourselves."

Giraud led the way to a room at the rear of the house. Here, on long trestle tables, half a dozen of Giraud's group were sifting through the piles of rubbish brought from the warehouse.

McCarter wandered along the tables, idly poking among the piles of rubbish. He moved on, then paused and went back to a spot where he had been checking. He began to search a little more thoroughly, looking for something that had caught his eye. He found what he was looking for and held it up, examining it carefully.

"Kaplan," he called.

Katz, with Giraud close behind, returned to where the Briton was standing.

"What is it?" Giraud asked.

McCarter held out the crumpled wrapping. It was a piece about four inches square.

"Recognize it?" the Brit asked Katz.

The Israeli nodded.

"C-4 wrapper," he said.

"Military plastic explosive," McCarter explained. "Consists of ninety percent Hexogen, better known as RDX, and ten percent polyisobutylene plasticizer. It's one of the most powerful explosives ever made. A ball the size of my fist would destroy this house. Until you put in the detonator it's perfectly harmless. Arm it and it becomes extremely dangerous."

"This is part of a U.S. Army wrapper," Katz said. "Looks like someone has been hijacking military supplies."

"So now we have Libyans. A missing ship. Plastic explosive," Giraud said. "I get the feeling we'd better locate that damned freighter pretty quickly."

MANNING RETURNED with Encizo, and the Cuban reported his conversation with Grimaldi back at Stony Man.

"I gave them all the information we had," Encizo explained. "They were going to get back to me."

Katz indicated a telephone. "You'd better call them. Give them our new location. Then let me speak to Hal."

McCarter told Manning and Encizo about the C-4 wrapper they had found, and he also updated them regarding the Libyans' ship.

When Encizo got through to Stony Man, Katz went on the line and spoke directly to Hal Brognola. The Fed sounded tired. Most likely he hadn't been to bed since the mission had got under way.

Brognola listened in silence as Katz related the most recent events.

"At least the Soviets are out of the picture for the present," Brognola said. "Tell Lomas I'm glad Karen wasn't hurt."

"Will do," Katz affirmed. "Our next priority is locating that ship. We haven't figured out what the Libyans are after. But it's obvious they're set on causing some outrage."

"The Bear should have some answers for you shortly. He's running a trace on the *Palomar*, trying to find out who really owns her. I'll feed him this new info about the C-4, and get him to look into any other related incidents."

"Make it fast, Hal," Katz said.

Giraud came in with a sheet of paper. There was a triumphant smile on his face.

"We have it," he said. "The *Palomar* gave her destination as Trieste. She has a cargo to pick up there in three days. She should arrive sometime during Friday."

"Still doesn't give us much help figuring out a possible target," Manning said. "The Libyans could be after something or someone between here and Trieste. Or a target in Trieste itself."

"Or something at sea," Encizo suggested.

"Difficult to try and outguess them," Manning observed. "Minds like theirs aren't exactly logical."

"Try and work out who's upset them lately," McCarter offered.

Calvin James came in to join them. "Those Russians were hard mothers," he said. "Resisted the scopolamine every inch of the way. Say what you like about them, but they've been trained well when it comes to holding back information."

"Did they give you anything?" Katz asked.

"A little."

"Well?" McCarter persisted.

"One did some mumbling about helicopters. The only other thing I got from another one was a single word. *Aviano.*"

"Sounds Italian," Manning said.

"It is," Giraud confirmed. "There is an American Air Force base at Aviano."

"That could be the target," Katz said. "The Libyans have been threatening reprisal for the bombing of Tripoli ever since it happened. One thing Khaddafi does have is a long memory and plenty of patience."

The Israeli snatched up the telephone and dialed the number that would put him back in contact with Stony Man. When Brognola came on the line, Katz spoke immediately.

"We have a possible target," he explained. "One of the KGB captives came up with a place name while under the influence of scopolamine. Aviano. We've confirmed it as the site of a U.S. airbase."

"Damned right it is," the Stony Man Fed replied. "I can add to that, Kaplan. The U.S. Secretary of Defence is on a European tour at the moment. Part of his itinerary is to be unpublicized visits to a number of NATO bases, for goodwill and morale apparently. I've only just been given this information. It was planned a couple of months ago. Nothing given out to anyone. Obviously there's been a leak somewhere. You won't be surprised to hear that one of the bases selected for a visit is Aviano. The secretary is scheduled to be there some time during Friday morning. He will leave Aviano just before noon."

"The same day our Libyans' ship arrives in the area," Katz said. "You'd better arrange for the secretary to change his schedule. But try to keep it quiet. We still have a bunch of Libyan terrorists and a ship loaded with C-4. Those hotheads are liable to explode their homemade bomb anywhere they might happen to be if they find out their target has got away. We have to locate and stop them."

"How do you expect to do that?" Brognola inquired. "Row out and ask them to heave to?"

"Can you find out if there are any U.S. Navy submarines in the area?" Katz asked. "Then arrange for them to give us a ride?"

"Now what crazy scheme are you hatching?" the Fed demanded, not really wanting to know the answer.

"Tell you later. Did the Bear come up with anything further?"

"Couple of items. There was a large theft of C-4 from a government warehouse in the Southwest. About three months back. Whoever arranged the heist knew what they were looking for. Didn't touch anything else in the place. Just moved the explosive and plenty of detonators. They took enough to level a small town, Katz. On to the *Palomar*—we've managed to trace ownership back as far as a company based in Paris. The main man is an Arab named Akar. We do know Akar. He's a personal friend and supporter of Khaddafi."

"It all fits neatly together," Katz mused. "Too well to be coincidence. I think we have enough to move on the *Palomar*. Find me a submarine, Hal. We need to reach that ship while she's out at sea."

"Stay close to a phone, Kaplan."

Giraud had a large ocean chart spread out across a table. He was tracing a line across it with a red pen, marking what he guessed would be the *Palomar*'s logical course.

"Taking into account the time she left, I would expect her to be somewhere around this area," he said. "How do you think they plan to carry out their plan?"

"From what we've learned," Katz began, "I'd guess they have a helicopter on board the *Palomar*. It will probably be of a type used by the U.S. Air Force. Most likely one that has been stolen or provided by a sympathetic regime. It will have been painted in correct USAF colors and markings. The interior will be packed with C-4, wired to detonate on impact. When the ship reaches the Italian coast in line with the Aviano air base, the helicopter will lift off and fly inland. Its time of arrival at the base will be timed to coincide with the visit of the Secretary of Defence. The helicopter flies over the base and is aimed like a bomb at a preselected target area. That area will be chosen so maximum damage and loss of life will be sustained. There would be a lot of top brass at the base. Plus U.S. base personnel."

"The way you tell it makes it sound too easy," James said.

"It could be just that," Katz replied. "A USAF helicopter won't be an unusual sight in the area. How often do you see a helicopter passing overhead? Fairly frequently. The ordinary man in the street wouldn't take that much notice. Even at the base, a chopper with Air Force markings isn't going to cause too much of a stir. By the time anyone figured this one should not be where it is, it would be too late."

"Let me know if you need anything when the time comes," Giraud offered.

"Right now some food would go down nicely," McCarter said, ever practical.

"For once the man has got it right," James agreed.

20

The Lafayette class missile submarine, powered by a nuclear reactor, was capable of doing thirty knots when submerged. The interior was much more comfortable than Phoenix Force had imagined. It was also quieter. As the submarine had been designed for long voyages while submerged, the quality of life for the crew had been taken into account.

The Force had been quartered in a briefing room and issued sleeping bags. There were no empty cabins on a submarine while on active service. The full complement of the crew occupied all the official cabin space.

The Stony Man warriors didn't complain. They had plenty to occupy them during the voyage. There were weapons to ready. Equipment to check. Their plan of action to formulate.

The call had come quickly from Stony Man. There *was* a U.S. submarine in the vicinity. A top-priority call had been relayed from Washington, diverting the vessel from its normal patrol. A rendezvous point had been arranged. Giraud, true to his word, had organized a power launch. He had piloted the launch himself, taking the Force out to the meeting with the submarine. The Navy had been on time. The sleek, dark form of the submarine rose from the depths amid a silver swell of bubbles. Within five minutes the vessel was submerging once again, leaving Giraud alone in the motor launch, bobbing gently on the ocean swell.

The commander of the submarine had his orders and carried them out with strict efficiency. He had been given the *Palomar*'s intended course, her speed and time of departure. From that, he and his navigation officer were able to work out the ship's position.

"We'll have to push to the limit," the commander said to Katz. "But we haven't lost a race yet, Mr. Kaplan. You and your men just sit tight. I'll give you a call when it's time."

The Phoenix warriors completed their equipment checks, donned their black combat suits and settled down for the long wait.

As a group they were coping with feeling incomplete due to Encizo's absence. The Cuban had also been affected by the parting from his partners. Phoenix Force had been together for a long time. They had been through many dangerous encounters, and all of them had suffered wounds of varying degrees along the way. None of them enjoyed the thought of sitting out a mission while the others carried on. Even when the reason for staying behind was totally justified, a member of the Force felt that he was letting his partners down and that his absence put them at risk. The truth usually was the opposite. The injured member would have added to the risk factor by staying with the team. The others might have suffered a lapse of concentration worrying about the wounded man. If that happened in the heat of a firefight, the consequences might prove fatal.

Despite the common-sense decision, the whole of the Force felt deprived of something.

While the submarine plowed its way through the depths of the Mediterranean, Phoenix Force rested. They slept, catching up on the hours they had missed since arriving in France. If they were not asleep, they sat in quiet repose, minds occupied with thoughts of what lay ahead or about the events of the past hectic hours.

The image of Leoni Testarov haunted Katz. He kept recalling that final moment in the villa when he had encountered the KGB man. In the frantic heat of the moment, when he and the Russian had been face-to-face, had there been an expression of resignation in Testarov's eyes? A look that admitted the man's acceptance of defeat? Katz could not swear to it. Yet there was that feeling lurking at the back of his mind. Had Testarov, despite all his planning, realized that his approach had been wrong? That his strategy had allowed Phoenix Force to gain the upper hand. Had it been such thoughts that had slowed Testarov's response? Acknowledging that he had failed in his second attempt to destroy Phoenix Force, perhaps Testarov had chosen a swift death over the fate that possibly awaited him on his return to Moscow.

Katz stirred restlessly, then pushed himself to his feet and crossed to the ever-ready coffee percolator to pour himself a mug. He stood, drinking the rich, black coffee and washing away the morbid thoughts.

The appearance of Martin Kohler in the game had been a shock for the Force. The realization that Reiger had worked and fought alongside them, got to know them was more than disconcerting. His closeness during the German mission would have provided him with excellent profiles of Phoenix Force. It was information he would have been able to pass to his KGB masters back in Moscow. Even if Reiger was dead, just what kind of information had he left as his legacy? Possibly details that might be of use in the future to the Soviet terror machine. The kind of information used to pinpoint Karen Hoffe and her association with Gary Manning. The KGB would guard their file zealously.

THE ARTIFICIAL ATMOSPHERE in the submarine gave no indication of day or night, and inactivity added to the sense of timelessness.

McCarter had found a pack of playing cards. He sat at the table playing solitaire.

A well-thumbed sports magazine provided Manning with some degree of distraction.

Katz sat beside James, discussing the merits of different types of submarine. The black Phoenix warrior had some experience of the undersea craft from his time as a SEAL in Vietnam.

There was a tap on the door. It opened to admit the commander's aide. "We have a sighting, gentlemen," he said. "Mr. Kaplan, would you join the commander at the control room? He would like you to take a look through the scope."

Katz followed the young officer through to the submarine's control room. It was a maze of technical equipment. Crew members went about their appointed tasks with professional ease. The scene was made slightly unreal by the subdued light that threw a red cast over everything.

The commander glanced around as Katz was led to him.

"We've made better time than we expected," he said. "Your ship has reduced speed. Could be she's ahead of schedule, so they've slowed down. Bit of luck for us."

Katz stepped up to the periscope. He placed his eyes to the rubber surround. There, in the graying light of early dawn, was the freighter. They were astern of her, and although the image in the scope was constantly rising and falling, Katz was able to read the name painted across the curved stern.

Palomar.

"Now would seem a good time to make your attempt," the commander said. "Still a while before full light. Most of the crew will be off watch. Catch them now, before they hit the decks."

"We're ready to go," Katz said.

"Best I can do is surface the conning tower and let you out with a couple of inflatables. She's still moving at a fairly good clip, and I can't get in too close in case we collide. You might have to do some hard paddling to reach her before she pulls ahead, but I think you'll manage it."

"Thanks for your help, commander," Katz said.

"We'll submerge and keep you in sight. If everything goes to plan, fire a signal flare and we'll surface and pick you up."

"And if we fail?" Katz asked, his curiosity getting the better of him.

"There are orders to cover such an eventuality. However, they are only to be used as an extreme measure. We have to be careful here. Without physical proof of what the people on board that ship intend doing, we can't touch her."

"I understand," Katz said. "We will get ready to leave."

He returned to the others. They were already prepared.

"Let's do it," Katz declared, picking up his gear and weapons.

THE DARK CONNING TOWER of the submarine broke the surface. The hull of the *Palomar* was little more than fifty feet off.

The side hatch was opened. A pair of inflatables, manhandled by crew members, were lowered by ropes into the water. The light rubber craft bounced across the surface of the ocean, buffeted by the movement of the submarine.

Katz and McCarter emerged from the hatch first. They used ropes attached to metal hooks to ease themselves down the rounded hull of the submarine and into one of the inflatables. Once they were in, they pulled the paddles from rubber loops and dug them into the water. The crewmen freed the ropes. The inflatable jerked away from the side of the submarine, spinning briefly before the Phoenix warriors got it under control. Then they began paddling, pushing to the craft toward the dark bulk of the *Palomar*.

The commander of the submarine had broken the surface toward the bow of the ship and had held his position there. That gave the Phoenix pair the opportunity to cross the gap before the ship drew ahead of them. Even so, Katz and McCarter were dripping with sweat as they neared the hull of the *Palomar*. With a final burst of effort they paddled the inflatable against the hull. McCarter had a line ready. Attached to the end was a powerful magnet-clamp, provided by the Navy. McCarter lifted the heavy block of metal and thrust it against the hull. He felt the magnet drag from his hand and stick itself to the metal. The Brit quickly fixed the free end of the rope to a thick towing loop at the front of the inflatable. He turned and gave the thumbs-up sign to Katz.

Manning and James had already set out on their crossing from the submarine. They pushed their rubber craft through the churning water, almost losing their forward motion in the wake of a heavy swell. Sheer determination pushed them on.

As Manning and James fell in behind, Katz tossed them a rope already tied to his craft. Manning caught it and used the rope to draw James and himself up close behind Katz and McCarter.

Glancing back, the Phoenix team saw that the submarine had already submerged. They were alone on the sea with the enemy ship and all its crew.

James unwound a coil of rope from around his shoulders. On the end of the rope was a three-pronged grappling hook. The curved metal prongs were covered in a layer of thin rubber to deaden any sound the hook made when striking a metal object.

Leaning out from the inflatable, James stared up the side of the ship. He was able to make out the metal rail edging the deck. He gauged the distance, swung the hook and released it. The metal prongs sailed up toward the rail, losing their momentum before reaching the rail.

James re-coiled the rope. He set himself and tried again. This time the hooks cleared the rail, striking the deck with a faint thud. James drew in the slack. He felt the hooks catch, so he gave the rope a snap, pulling the hooks tight against whatever they had snagged. Again leaning out from the inflatable for a better view, he could see that the rope was angling out from the top of the rail. He put more pressure on the rope to ensure that it had really got a hold. Satisfied, he nodded to the others.

Bracing his feet against the hull of the ship, James pulled himself hand over hand up the side. The rope was knotted every foot, enabling whoever was climbing to maintain a good grip.

As his head reached the level of the deck, James paused in his climb. He gripped the rail and drew himself close, peering through the gap. He checked the deck area in both directions and saw nothing. He quickly scrambled over the rail and onto the *Palomar*'s deck. Then he leaned over and tugged on the rope for the next man to make the climb.

Manning pulled himself swiftly up the rope and dropped to the deck beside James. The Canadian stood guard while James tugged on the rope again.

Standing ready, Katz looped the rope around his waist and waved his hand to James. While Katz walked up the side of the ship, James hauled in the slack. It was one of the few occasions when the Israeli had to depend on others for help. Once he was on deck, he would become his totally independent self again.

With Katz on board, the rope was dropped for McCarter. He scrambled up to the rail and swung his legs to the deck. The rope was pulled in, and the grappling hook freed from the rail. It was pushed out of sight under a metal stanchion.

The four Phoenix warriors drew into the shadows thrown by a metal companionway as they discussed their next move.

"We need to confirm our suspicions about the helicopter," Katz said. "According to Giraud, the largest of the cargo holds is toward the bow."

"Is that the pointed bit?" McCarter asked dryly, and James gave him a quick jab in the ribs.

"We'll try and work our way in that direction," Katz went on. "Remember one thing. These Libyans have to be pretty extreme to be planning this attack. That means they are not going to be best pleased at us showing up."

"I think he means they're a bunch of fanatics and they'll be bloody pissed off," McCarter translated, mainly for his own benefit.

"We get the message," Manning said. "These guys genuinely believe they're on a holy crusade for Allah. Whatever we think about them, *they* know they're in the right. There's no rational discussion of the problem with them."

"Okay," James agreed. "We are knee-deep in hostile territory. We'll handle any problems if they come our way. In the meantime, what do we do if we come across the helicopter?"

"Tread bloody carefully," McCarter suggested. "What about trying to disable it? That'll knock their scheme on the head."

"Good idea," Katz said. "Let's go and see if we can find it."

They were situated about midway along the *Palomar*'s deck. They had over two hundred feet to cover before they reached the cargo hold. The main superstructure provided cover for the first fifty to sixty feet. Beyond that, the main deck lay fairly open, with some cover available in the form of winches and odds and ends of equipment strewn about.

Katz led the way, with James bringing up the rear. The Phoenix quartet checked every shadow and watched every companionway and hatch as they neared them. They were acutely aware of their precarious position. Liable to be discovered at any given moment by an enemy of extreme behavior, they could easily find themselves in a dead-end situation. They did not know the odds they might be facing, nor the skill of their potential opponents.

Reaching the end of the superstructure, they halted in the shadows as they studied the area before them.

"Over there," Manning whispered.

He indicated the dark outline of a man on the opposite side of the ship, moving along the deck. The figure was in silhouette, with a weapon in his hands.

Katz scanned their side of the deck. He picked out the objects that would offer them cover as they traveled the next hundred feet.

"Have to do it in stages," he instructed. "Cover me."

The Israeli darted forward, keeping low as he approached a heavy winch.

He had two paces to go, two paces that would have taken him to the safety of the winch. But at the moment he commenced the first of those steps, a figure loomed into view, having just ascended a companionway from below decks.

Katz was caught out in the open. Exposed in the pale, clearing light of the new dawn.

The man on the companionway looked into the Israeli's face, and failing to recognize the man, understood that this stranger was not a Libyan—and therefore had to be an enemy.

The Arab broke his trance quickly and grabbed for the AK-74 hanging from his shoulder. At the same time, he let out a bloodcurdling yell at the top of his voice.

Seconds later the crackle of an automatic weapon shattered the dawn silence.

21

The Libyan's AK-74 spat 5.45 mm steel-cored slugs.
Katz, anticipating the Arab's reaction, had turned
his body aside just ahead of the terrorist's trigger
pull. He felt the hot path of the projectiles, heard
them clang against the ship's steelwork. Then he was
lunging forward, bringing his right arm around in a
slashing drive. The curving steel hooks of his prosthesis gouged flesh, tearing across the Arab's face.
The man screamed and fell back in shock. His withdrawal gave Katz the time he needed to bring his Uzi
into play. The SMG ripped out a short burst, planting a cluster of slugs in the Arab's chest that drove
him to the deck.

The short outburst of firing acted as a signal, and
within seconds the ship was in an uproar as raised
voices echoed back and forth.

An alarm bell began to shrill and add its urgency
to the din.

Katz, aware that all need for caution had gone
overboard, turned and waved to the rest of his team.
He found they were already on the move, breaking
cover to join him.

Alerted by the racket, the guard they had spotted on the far side of the ship came running. As he rounded the bulk of a ventilator shaft, he ran into a stream of 9 mm slugs from McCarter's KG-99. The Libyan gave a startled grunt as the hot flesh-shredders tore into his chest. He continued to run forward until his legs went from under him and he crashed heavily to the deck.

"Go for that hold," Katz yelled.

A line of ferocious slugs marched across the deck, clanging against the plating.

Manning turned, raising the muzzle of the SA-80, tracking in on the gunman. The Canadian stroked the trigger, and his return fire sent a stream of bullets at the Libyan who was leaning out from a hatch on the main superstructure. Some of Manning's slugs bounced off the steelwork, and others thudded into the Arab's chest and face, destroying his flesh and his will to live in a blinding flash of pain. He flopped loosely out of the hatch.

As they ran along the deck, covering each other, the Phoenix warriors became aware of more armed men appearing. The Libyans seemed to be emerging from every hatch on the ship.

Calvin James turned his M-16 on a bunch who had burst from one of the hatches. He triggered a HE round from the M-203 grenade launcher. The round struck the deck just ahead of the Libyans, exploding with a crash. They were scattered like sand before the wind, their bodies shredded by the blast. Limp broken forms thudded to the deck, blood oozing from the lacerated flesh.

McCarter, close on Katz's heels, fired from the hip. He blew one screaming terrorist off his feet, then yanked the muzzle around to catch yet another figure, scything the terrorist's legs from under him. The Libyan smashed facedown on the deck, his head dissolving into a red mask of agony.

Autofire sent a stream of slugs over Katz's head. The bullets ripped into the wood of one of the ship's lifeboats. Katz half turned, his Uzi tracking in on the attacker. The terrorist, a stocky, dark Libyan, leaned out from behind a stack of fuel drums, the muzzle of his MP-5 lining up on Katz. The Israeli dropped to one knee, bracing the Uzi across his prosthesis. He triggered quickly, and 9 mm slugs tore jagged holes in one of the fuel drums. Aviation fuel spurted from the holes, splashing into the face of the terrorist. He drew back, coughing harshly and sleeving the liquid from his eyes. He was caught by Katz's second volley, the slugs tearing his throat open in a burst of red. The dying Libyan tumbled backward, his finger pulling tight on the MP-5's trigger and sending a stream of slugs into the fuel drums. Sparks from the slugs ignited the vapor from the fuel. The fuel burst into flame in an instant, spreading quickly. Katz ran forward, dropping to the deck moments before the drums exploded. A ball of fire rolled skyward as drums of fuel blew up off the deck like rockets. Some of them hurtled over the side of the ship, then dropped into the ocean, where they were extinguished.

Ignoring the blaze, McCarter planted his back against a steel bulkhead. He ejected the empty magazine from his KG-99 and pulled a fresh one from his ammo pockets. He clicked it into place. Before he had time to cock the weapon, he was confronted by a wild-eyed man wielding a long knife. The terrorist was half-dressed and barefoot. He had been woken from sleep and had rushed into the fray armed only with his knife. He lunged at McCarter. The Briton swayed back from the keen blade, then lashed out with his right fist. His knuckles caught the Libyan across the bridge of the nose, crushing the thin bones. Blood gushed from the man's nostrils, dripping onto his naked chest. But the pain did not deter him. He slashed the knife back and forth, forcing McCarter to retreat. McCarter felt his heels catch something and a moment later he went down on his back. Seeing an opportunity to finish off his enemy, the Libyan drove forward. McCarter drew his legs up and back, then smashed them into the Libyan's body. He thrust hard, sending the terrorist crashing into a steel upright. McCarter rolled to his feet, snatching the Browning Hi-Power from his shoulder rig. He aimed, then let loose two 9 mm slugs that burrowed into the ridge between the terrorist's eyes. The Libyan threw his arms wide and sagged to the deck.

Up on the catwalk that ran around the bridge, a pair of terrorists had set up the M-60 machine gun. The loader fed in the belt of 7.62 mm ammunition. The gunner arced the weapon on its swivel, searching for the black-clad invaders who seemed to have come out of nowhere. He spotted one of them, a tall, lanky black man, and opened fire. The 7.62 mm slugs hammered from the M-60's muzzle, leaving bright score marks in the metal deck plates but falling short of the intended target.

James felt the steel plates vibrate underfoot as they were pounded by the 7.62 mm slugs. He turned and caught a glimpse of the machine gun position before he ducked out of range. Staying behind the power winch, James pulled an M-406 HE round from his combat harness and loaded it into the grenade launcher. With the weapon ready to fire, he leaned out from behind the winch, the M-16 to his shoulder. Aiming carefully, James pulled the trigger. He watched the round curve its way toward the bridge. The round cleared the top of the catwalk and struck the bulkhead just behind the machine gun crew. It exploded on impact, shattering windows in the bridge bulkhead and showering the terrorists with its deadly load of 325 fragments. In the close area of the catwalk, the terrorists took the full brunt of the explosion. The sizzling fragments tore them to bloody shreds.

Immediately after he had fired the grenade, James sensed movement to his right and twisted in that direction. A Libyan lunged at him, aiming an automatic pistol. James swore in frustration as he attempted to bring the M-16 into play. The Libyan fired first. James felt a burning pain across his right side. He lashed out with his right leg, catching the man on the ankles and knocking him to the deck.

James scrambled to his feet. He swung the stock of the rifle against the Libyan's jaw, smashing him to the deck. The Libyan snarled in rage, spitting blood. He tried to bring his pistol into play again. James kicked out and his boot whacked the terrorist full in the face. The Libyan flopped back against the deck, his skull crunching as he struck. His body arched, arms and legs twitching for a time, before he gave a final shudder and became still.

James put a hand to his side. He felt warm blood oozing through the tear in his combat suit. His ribs felt sore, as well, but there was no stabbing pain, so he didn't think there were any broken. But there wasn't much to be done just then, so he turned back to the firefight.

Manning reached the cargo hold. He saw that the covers were in place. A quick searching glance revealed an access ladder that led below decks. When bullets splattered against the deck plating, Katz moved alongside the Canadian. He drove back a trio of advancing Libyans with a long burst from his Uzi. The group scattered, giving the Phoenix pros brief seconds of freedom. "Get down there," Katz said. "I'll cover for you."

"Watch yourself," Manning said, then swung his legs over the ladder access and began his descent.

Katz crouched by the cargo hold, shielded by the raised sides. He put in a fresh magazine of 9 mms into the Uzi and cocked the SMG.

He heard the sounds of battle from other parts of the ship. That meant McCarter and James were still holding their own against the terrorists.

MANNING REACHED the bottom of the ladder. He found himself in a square room adjacent to the main hold. A large extractor unit, used to draw fumes and dust from the hold, took up most of the space. To the right was an open hatch that led into the main hold. He turned and crossed to the hatch, ready to step through, then paused.

He spotted someone move on the other side of the hatch, and reacted instinctively, pulling back from the open hatch. A heavy blast of autofire followed. Bullets struck the steel frame of the hatch, ricocheting with vicious whines.

Crouching, Manning peered around the lower frame. The hold was in semidarkness, pools of light contrasting with the dense shadows.

He scanned the area, watching, waiting. His patience was rewarded when he saw his man step out of the shadows. The guy was dark skinned, with wild, angry eyes. He carried an AK-74 in his hands.

Manning pulled the SA-80 into position and fired the moment he had the terrorist in his sights. The 5.56 mm slugs slammed the guy off his feet. He crashed to the floor of the hold, squirming around in the shadows. For a while a tirade of Arabic poured from the Libyan's lips, then abruptly the man fell silent.

The moment he had fired, Manning slipped through the door, ducking low and merging with the pools of darkness at the base of the hold.

As his eyes adjusted to the gloom, Manning made out the bulky dark mass in the middle of the hold. It quickly formed into the outline of a helicopter with its rotor blades collapsed and tied in position along the length of the tail. Manning recognized the craft as a Bell JetRanger. It was in USAF livery, complete with insignia.

They had guessed right, after all!

Manning eased away from the side of the hold, wanting to get a better look at the chopper. He was certain that he would find the passenger compartment filled with C-4 explosive.

He reached the rear of the JetRanger and cautiously made his way along the tail section. The cabin section came in view. Manning moved along it until he was able to peer in through the side window.

The entire cabin section was jammed with C-4 blocks. They were stacked to the ceiling of the compartment and backed up to the pilot's seat. He could also see the wires running from the C-4 to the front of the compartment. Manning stepped to the front hatch. There on the pilot's seat lay the ends of the wires leading from the detonators. They were not yet connected up to the electronic detonating unit lying on the seat.

The Canadian located the engine cover. He loosened the fasteners with the blade of his knife and deposited it on the floor. He stared into the depths of the engine.

"Well, Gary, this is no time to be indecisive."

He leaned his SA-80 against one of the outriggers, reached into the compartment and tore free every cable he could lay his hands on. The thick blade of his knife cut through a couple of aluminum tubes, allowing fluid to spurt free.

Turning to the helicopter, Manning yanked opened the pilot's hatch. He reached in and picked up the detonating unit. He tossed it to the floor and crushed it with his boot.

Manning then swiftly retraced his steps, returned to the metal ladder and climbed up out of the hold. He cleared the top of the hatch and rolled out onto the deck while managing to press himself close to the raised sides of the hold.

The firefight still raged around him, and flames from the burning fuel drums continued to lick across the deck.

A hand grabbed Manning's sleeve. He turned and stared into Katz's face. The Israeli dragged him around the far side of the hold.

"Just as we figured," the Canadian said. "Helicopter in USAF livery. Packed out with C-4. I disabled the chopper and destroyed the detonator."

"Good," Katz said. "Now all we have to do is a clean-up operation and get the hell off this tub."

Manning looked up and saw a group of Libyans bursting out from the cabin area below the bridge. They were yelling wildly as they charged toward the Phoenix commandos.

"I can appreciate what Custer must have felt like," the Canadian remarked as he tracked in on the massed attack.

22

When the first shots had broken the early-morning calm, Rashid had been going over the details of the operation again with a fine-tooth comb.

He snatched up his Beretta 12S SMG and ran to the door of the cabin. He threw it open and stepped out onto the bridge section. Calling to one of his aides, he moved to the front of the bridge and stared down at the deck.

A furious firefight had broken out. His Libyan warriors were striking at a number of black-clad figures who had somehow appeared on board. Rashid had no idea how the attackers had got on the ship. The only rational explanation was that they had stowed away before the *Palomar* had left Marseilles. Even that explanation failed to ring true. The ship had been checked from stem to stern before sailing. And it had been a thorough search. Not only that, but there had been armed guards on board the ship during its stay in the French dock. So that still posed the question—how had the raiders got on board?

Rashid decided that it was a question he had to leave until later. The most important consideration was the elimination of the attackers. There was too much at stake to allow the operation to be jeopardized at such a late stage. Time and effort and expense had been poured into the project, and while none of those things mattered in the end, more than enough resources had been expended to even allow thoughts of failure. As far as Rashid was concerned, failure was a word he refused to recognize. This project had been his from the moment of conception. His outrage at the Americans' unprovoked and cowardly attack on his native land did more than anything else to convince him that the war against the U.S.A. had to continue. As the months passed and no retribution was meted out to the Americans, Rashid began to formulate his plan. The air base at Aviano was chosen because of its comparative closeness to a coastal area and because it had been the American Air Force that had carried out the bombing raid on Tripoli. The *Palomar*, which belonged to the Libyans, was chosen as the carrier of the helicopter. Due to its being seen regularly in the majority of ports along the Spanish-French-Italian coastline, no one would even suspect it of being involved in any unlawful venture. The appearance of the Russians in Marseilles had come as a bonus. They had been able to furnish a safehouse and had also provided technical advice concerning the explosive charges in the helicopter. When the Russians had come under attack from some renegade American murder squad, Rashid had become uneasy. He wanted nothing to interfere with his plan. He decided to advance the sailing of the *Palomar*. Once clear of Marseilles and far out at sea, they could finalize their preparations without fear of interference. All had been going smoothly... until now.

"How many are there?" he demanded from one of his men.

The Libyan shrugged. "There has been no time for counting," he replied. "These madmen are killing us all."

Rashid rounded on the man angrily. "That is the talk of a defeatist. A coward."

"No, Rashid, it is the talk of a realist."

Rashid pushed him out of the way and headed for the companionway that led to the deck area. He hurried along the deck, thrusting his way through a hatch. He ran along the passage to the large cabin where the main bulk of his squad was housed. When he burst through the entryway, he saw that they were already up and arming themselves.

"We are under attack," Rashid said. "A number of your comrades have already paid the price for defending our faith. They must not be allowed to die for nothing. Arm yourselves and come with me. Let us be rid of these murderers."

He thrust his SMG over his head. *"For the holy war,"* he screamed. *"For Allah and the glory of Islam."*

The others took up the chant, working themselves into a fury of religious fervor. Thoughts of personal danger were wiped away by the possibility of dying for Allah and reaching the paradise his worshippers had been promised.

Rashid held open the door and urged his men forward. They streamed out of the cabin and made for the hatchway that would take them out onto the deck of the *Palomar*.

23

"I get the feeling these blokes aren't ready to listen to reason," McCarter said.

James, watching the advancing horde of Libyans, couldn't hold back a smile at the Briton's words.

"Do tell," he replied.

The leading terrorists opened fire, spraying the area with 5.45 mm bullets. The heavy barrage sent a stream of projectiles in the general direction of Phoenix Force. It was more of a diversion than anything else, designed to keep the Stony Man warriors under cover as the Libyans advanced.

Phoenix Force, as usual, refused to play according to the rules. Instead of diving for cover and staying put, they hit back.

"David, cover me," James said as he loaded a HE round into the grenade launcher.

McCarter fired off a long burst from his KG-99, knocking a pair of Libyans off their feet as they moved closer than the rest of the group. Their comrades behind them slowed their assault, giving James time to trigger the HE round in their direction. It arced across the deck and landed just ahead of the main group. The blast eliminated three Libyans altogether, throwing their bloodied corpses across the deck. One struck the side rail of the ship and tumbled into the ocean.

Meanwhile, Katz and Manning had skirted along the outer edge of the hold, then angled around the still-burning fuel drums. The maneuver brought them close to the rear of the terrorists.

The exploding grenade had scattered the enemy, and a number of them decided to work their way around to the other side of the ship. That brought them face-to-face with Katz and Manning.

It was the burly Canadian who saw the Libyans first. Smoke from the burning fuel had drifted away momentarily and allowed Manning to make out the figures of armed men cutting across the deck.

"Visitors," he warned Katz.

The Israeli spotted the advancing Libyans. He and Manning raised their weapons, and as the Libyans broke free from the drifting smoke and recognized the Phoenix pair, the Stony Man commandoes opened fire.

Katz planted a trio of 9 mm slugs in the chest of one terrorist, slamming the man to the deck. He swiveled his Uzi instantly and triggered a second time, catching his target in the upper thigh as the Libyan made a valiant effort to escape his fate. The terrorist went down, rolling desperately, trying to train his AK-74 on Katz. The Israeli had dropped into a crouch, tracking the wounded man and losing him when smoke wafted across his field of vision.

When he could see again, the Libyan had gained his feet and was in the act of firing. Katz pulled the Uzi's trigger. His bullets missed the terrorist, but they were close enough to make him hop to one side. He lost his balance and staggered, his AK-74 exploding with sound and sending its shots wide. The terrorist fell backward, letting out a scream as he crashed against the blazing fuel drums. He dislodged a number of the drums and slipped to his knees as they bounced across the deck, spilling more fuel across the steel plates. The next moment the fuel ignited, engulfing him in flames. His screams were lost in the roar of the flames and the general din of battle.

Another terrorist drew a bead on Gary Manning, pulling the trigger. He was rewarded by the sight of the Canadian stumbling as a bullet gouged a ragged furrow across his left thigh. The Libyan raised the muzzle of his assault rifle to fire a killing shot. The shot never came. Manning had allowed himself to drop to his knees but had kept both hands on his SA-80. He triggered the weapon, blasting 5.56 mm slugs in a continuous stream at the charging man. His first two shots missed, but by the third he had the Libyan in his sights. He saw his bullets hit home, blowing ragged holes in the terrorist's chest. The Libyan was turned sideways by the force of the bullets, and Manning caught a brief glimpse of the bloody holes in his back where the slugs had emerged. The Libyan's momentum carried him forward for another couple of yards before he crashed to the deck.

The moment he had dealt with his target, Manning turned his SA-80 on a bearded terrorist who was tracking Katz. Manning shouldered the SA-80, aiming and firing in a heartbeat. His twin projectiles drove deep into the Libyan's skull, bursting out the opposite side and giving the terrorist an early opportunity for entry into paradise.

McCarter and James had pressed forward with their attack, determined not to lose the advantage they had gained from the HE grenade. The moment the blast had cleared, the Phoenix pair broke cover and raced across the deck to confront the dazed Libyans. Neither of the Stony Man warriors hesitated, aware that the only way to keep the advantage was to take the fight directly to the terrorists.

James triggered his M-16 into a cluster of Libyans, cutting them to shreds with concentrated fire. The terrorists were flung to the deck in sprays of blood, their bodies twitching as they spilled their lives onto the steel plates of the *Palomar*. Hearing his rifle click empty, James snatched his Beretta 92-SB from its shoulder holster. He selected his targets, blasting shot after shot at the disoriented terrorists.

Only a few feet away, David McCarter, on full throttle, burst among the Libyans like an avenging angel, his KG-99 wreaking havoc. McCarter, oblivious to any personal danger, sent blast after blast into the terrorists. He saw them spin away, bodies torn and bloody, many with their weapons unfired. Others managed to get off ill-timed shots before the roaring Phoenix avenger cut them down. McCarter, his adrenaline boiling, didn't even notice the bullet that clipped his left upper arm or see the blood that began to spread across his combat suit. His full attention was on the yelling, screaming, wide-eyed Libyans, his only aim to stop them before they stopped him. He heard the KG-99 snap empty. Swinging it one-handed, he lashed it across the face of a terrorist who appeared before him. The Libyan fell against the side rail, blood pouring from the deep gash in his face. He tried to raise the Beretta 12S SMG he carried, determined to kill the black-clad madman who had destroyed so many of his men. But by then, McCarter had drawn his Browning Hi-Power. He swung it around and triggered three quick shots into the Libyan's chest. The 9 mm rounds crashed through muscle and bone, cleaving the terrorist's heart. Coughing blood, the man slumped to the deck.

McCarter was not even aware that he had just killed Rashid, the driving force behind the Libyan group.

He turned away, triggering the Browning into the howling face of yet another terrorist. The face exploded into a scarlet mass.

The British ace dropped to a crouch, the muzzle of his gun arcing back and forth, seeking another target. All he saw was Calvin James, whose own handgun was probing the air.

It took a few long seconds for them both to realize there were no targets left.

Then Katz and Manning emerged from the drifting smoke of the burning fuel. Manning was limping from a leg wound. His combat suit was soaked in blood.

The Phoenix warriors stood in a group and surveyed the carnage around them.

Many of the Libyans were dead. Some were wounded, but definitely out of the fight.

The only survivor above decks was the ship's captain. Throughout the battle he had stayed at the wheel, keeping the *Palomar* on course. There would be others down in the engine room. Phoenix Force had no intention of harming them as long as they maintained their present status.

Katz observed the wounds James, McCarter and Manning had sustained. Adding Encizo's injury meant that only he, Katz, had come through unscathed.

"Seeing as I'm the only one fit and well," the Israeli said, "I'd better go tell the captain to stop the engines and drop the anchor. Can you guys manage on your own for a while?"

McCarter made a rude noise, and Katz chuckled as he walked away.

"Not bad for an old man," he said just loudly enough for the others to hear.

THREE HOURS LATER the Force watched the *Palomar* dwindle in the distance as the submarine moved away.

During those three hours a great deal of activity had taken place on board the ship. Once the captain had cut the engines and dropped anchor, he and his remaining crew had been herded into a cabin below decks and secured to bunks. The single porthole had been sealed off from the outside. Then all the wounded Libyans had been carried to another cabin, again one in which the porthole had been secured. Up on deck Katz had signaled to the watching submarine. Once his signal had been spotted through the submerged craft's periscope, the submarine had surfaced and come alongside. Members of the crew had come aboard. Medics, clad in plain, unmarked coveralls, had tended to the wounded and made them as comfortable as possible. Meanwhile engineers from the submarine had opened the cargo hold. Using the *Palomar*'s deck machinery, they had lifted the helicopter up out of the hold. The C-4 explosive had been removed and transferred to the submarine, and the helicopter had been dumped in the ocean.

After having their wounds seen to, McCarter, James and Manning had joined Katz in a search of the ship. They had eventually located the cabin used by the Libyan terrorist in charge of the mission. There they found the proof that pointed the finger at the Libyans. The plan of action, a detailed map of Aviano air base and a timetable plotting the Secretary of Defence's movements during his visit to the base. There were other documents in Arabic that would probably incriminate the Libyans even further. Katz gathered all the documentation and took it with him. It would be handed over when they got back to Stony Man.

Before Phoenix Force returned to the submarine, Katz went down to the cabin where the captain and his crewmen were secured. He left the keys to the handcuffs securing the Libyans on a table. Next he proceeded to free the captain. "You understand English?" Katz asked.

The man looked at him soberly and nodded.

"Then listen. We are leaving now. Your wounded have received medical treatment. You will remain in this cabin for exactly one hour. After that, you may free your men and go wherever you decide. Do not come up on deck before that hour is up. Believe me when I say we will be watching. If you ignore my words, we won't hesitate to sink this ship. We could have killed you all, but we are not murderers. We only fight those who intend us harm. You haven't done anything, so we do not intend harming you. But show yourself before the end of the hour, and we will take it as a hostile act. Then your ship will be destroyed with everyone aboard."

The captain had seen the fighting spirit of the commandos, and he had no desire to incur their wrath. "You have my word," he said. "Thank you for tending to the injured. May Allah be with you."

Katz looked at the man and believed his intent. He simply nodded and walked out of the cabin, closing the door behind him.

The Navy men had already returned to the submarine, and Katz and the others joined them. The rubber inflatables were taken back aboard the sub, hatches were closed and the craft eased away from the *Palomar*. As soon as the ship had been cleared, the commander instructed everyone to enter the submarine. Once the conning tower hatch was secure, the submarine slid gracefully beneath the waves. The course was set, and the sleek undersea craft turned about and headed home.

EPILOGUE

Nikolai Gagarin finished reading the long and detailed report. He sighed wearily, then tossed the file across his desk. He sat in contemplative silence, staring out of the window. From his office he could only see empty sky. Pale blue sky, with only a few shreds of clouds showing. He knew that it was a pleasant day outside. So why then did it feel cold in his office?

It was the chill wind of defeat, Gagarin knew. Leoni Testarov's defeat at the hands of the elusive American specialists tainted all who had been involved in the project. And that included Gagarin, as well. News of the loss had finally reached Moscow, and like all bad news, it had reached the ears of those who would have liked nothing better than the removal of the KGB completely. Fortunately for Gagarin and his colleagues, the KGB was still far too deeply entrenched in the Soviet infrastructure. The current humiliation would weaken their position, but it would be temporary. The KGB would weather it.

Gagarin's immediate concern was whether he personally could remain unscathed. Apart from the

KGB loss, there was the Libyan involvement. The U.S.S.R. was trying to integrate with the Islamic world. The Libyan connection had been one more attempt at extending the hand of friendship—albeit a furtive one. Not only had the American specialists wiped out Testarov and his force—they had then gone on and thwarted the Libyan's planned attack on the Aviano air base.

Rage shook Gagarin, and he smashed his fist on the top of his desk in pure frustration. What was it that made those Americans so invincible? They were only men, after all. He sat back, his anger subsiding. Men, yes. But *what* men. If he had a hundred like them he could . . . Gagarin shook his head. Now he was being stupid. The real world was not like that. Men such as the American specialists were not plucked from trees. Beyond their skill, they possessed a quality that was not something drilled into them. It was something they had breathed in with the very air in their country. An ideal they believed in so deeply it made them what they were.

Gagarin realized that if he had any chance of defeating them, he first had to find the source of their ideal. He needed to see inside their heads. First he had to observe how they performed and then analyze the force behind their deeds. Maybe then, when he understood the motivation, he could defeat them.

He stood up and crossed to the filing cabinet. After yanking open the top drawer, he removed a thick file and took it back to his desk.

The file contained all the information the KGB had on the team of specialists. Gagarin hoped that by absorbing every word before him he might begin his task of psyching out the American combat team on their next encounter.

He unloosened his tie, turned on the reading lamp by his side and sat back. Shutting all other concerns from his mind, he began to read.

TAKE 'EM NOW

FOLDING SUNGLASSES
FROM GOLD EAGLE

Mean up your act with these tough, street-smart shades. Practical, too, because they fold 3 times into a handy, zip-up polyurethane pouch that fits neatly into your pocket. Rugged metal frame. Scratch-resistant acrylic lenses. Best of all, they can be yours for only $6.99.

MAIL YOUR ORDER TODAY.

Offer not available in Canada.

Phoenix Force—bonded in secrecy to avenge the acts of terrorists everywhere

SEARCH AND DESTROY $3.95 ☐

American "killer" mercenaries are involved in a KGB plot to overthrow the government of a South Pacific island. The American President, anxious to preserve his country's image and not disturb the precarious position of the island nation's government, sends in the experts—Phoenix Force—to prevent a coup.

FIRE STORM $3.95 ☐

An international peace conference turns into open warfare when terrorists kidnap the American President and the premier of the USSR at a summit meeting. As a last desperate measure Phoenix Force is brought in—for if demands are not met, a plutonium core device is set to explode.

Total Amount	$ _____
Plus 75¢ Postage	_____ .75
Payment enclosed	$ _____

Please send a check or money order payable to Gold Eagle Books.

In the U.S.	In Canada
Gold Eagle Books	Gold Eagle Books
901 Fuhrmann Blvd.	P.O. Box 609
Box 1325	Fort Erie, Ontario
Buffalo, NY 14269-1325	L2A 5X3

Please Print

Name: _____

Address: _____

City: _____

State/Prov: _____

Zip/Postal Code: _____

SPF-A

Do you know a real hero?

At Gold Eagle Books we know that heroes are not just fictional. Everyday someone somewhere is performing a selfless task, risking his or her own life without expectation of reward.

Gold Eagle would like to recognize America's local heroes by publishing their stories. If you know a true to life hero (that person might even be you) we'd like to hear about him or her. In 150-200 words tell us about a heroic deed you witnessed or experienced. Once a month, we'll select a local hero and award him or her with national recognition by printing his or her story on the inside back cover of THE EXECUTIONER series, and the ABLE TEAM, PHOENIX FORCE and/or VIETNAM: GROUND ZERO series.

Send your name, address, zip or postal code, along with your story of 150-200 words (and a photograph of the hero if possible), and mail to:

LOCAL HEROES AWARD
Gold Eagle Books
225 Duncan Mill Road
Don Mills, Ontario
M3B 3K9
Canada